Willow

By G.L. Gracie

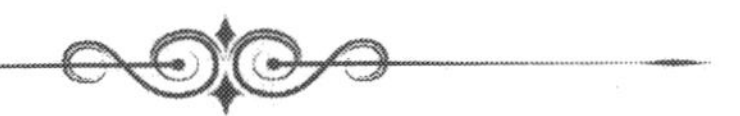

Hope & believe
Glenda

Willow
By G.L. Gracie

Formatting and Graphics by Leah Banicki

https://www.facebook.com/G.L.Gracie

Chapter One

It had been fifteen minutes since Mr. Carpenter rang the hand bell dismissing students from the little green shingled four room school house and sent them pouring into the country roads for the walk home. Noise of children laughing and playing echoed across the cooling October day.

Willow ran to catch up with her best friend, Alice, and the two chatted away as they scuffed the newly fallen autumn leaves with their shoes. Willow could feel the hole in the sole of her left shoe and wondered if there would ever be enough money for a new pair. Her dress was a cotton plaid and mother had done such a good job on the patches that probably nobody else would notice them. Pulling her sweater, which also had a patch on the left arm, to button it against the chill in the autumn air, she mused that Grandma Bessie would surely share some of her wisdom with her curt remark. *You'll catch your death if you don't button up that sweater.* Grandma Bessie always had a bit of wisdom to share with the young folks. Willow shifted the books in her arm and continued talking with Alice about their school day.

Alice was a good friend, Ivy's best friend, always bubbly and positive; but recent illness had left her pale and lethargic. Willow watched as Alice walked the path to her house and turned to wave and watched as the blonde braids disappeared behind the torn screen door. Alice's braids were always so neat and in place in contrast to Willow's unruly head of curls. Maybe she would ask mother if *her* curls could be braided. *Be content with what you have.* Grandma Bessie's words rang in her ears. But it was difficult for a young girl not to want some things, especially when there was so much to want for during these war years.

She adjusted the arithmetic book once again and felt the brown paper bag neatly folded inside it which had contained her meager lunch for the day. And it would not be thrown away because it would be used again tomorrow and for days after that. Maybe someday she could have a real lunch box, she mused as she saw fellow classmates up ahead of her. Connie Brown. Connie lived on the north side of the community in a really fine house. *She* had a metal lunch box. *Her* shoes didn't have holes in them and *her* dresses weren't patched. *She* always had matching bows in her hair and Willow had even seen a shiny store-bought red apple in her lunch box.

Connie's real name was Constance. Willow thought of her own name. Named after a tree, no less. She was embarrassed every time she heard it out loud. Except when Miss Tyler said it. Miss Tyler was her fifth grade teacher; and when Miss Tyler said her name, Willow thought it was a beautiful whisper. That was far from Mrs. White's rendition the previous year when Willow was in fourth grade. She was glad she didn't have to walk past Mrs. White's room this year to get to class.

Fourth grade had its issues. Peering over her spectacles which were always perched mid-way down her nose, Mrs. White was forever scolding Willow for daydreaming in class. The glasses at half-mast gave the teacher an ominous appearance and caused Willow to cringe with fear. Mrs. White's screeching voice still echoed in Willow's ears and she shuddered at the thought. Once when Willow was writing a poem about geese she'd seen heading south that morning on her way to school, Mrs. White had taken the paper from her and tore it and threw it in the waste basket. Miss Tyler wasn't like that. She encouraged Willow to write and Willow flourished under Miss Tyler's kindness.

Well, perhaps one day she'd change her name when she got older to something like Penelope or Grace or Meredith. Today, it was just about getting home and getting chores done and the arithmetic homework finished. Ugh! Willow loved to write and read and study history and draw and sing on occasion, but arithmetic was another thing. Her stomach tied knots inside itself when it was time for arithmetic. Arithmetic always came after morning recess. Terrible anticipation would begin when Willow heard the bell ring summoning students to form the two straight lines to enter the building. One line for boys. One line for girls. No talking or moving. No varying from the rules. Only then would students be allowed to return to their desks for the dreaded arithmetic class. Indeed, there were times when arithmetic had ruined a really good recess period.

Connie Brown was good at arithmetic. As a matter of fact, Connie Brown was good at everything. Oh, if only Willow had a beautiful name and beautiful clothes and could be smart like Connie Brown.

"Hey, Willow."

Willow was so lost in her own thoughts she hadn't heard Bobby Carson's bike come to a stop beside her.

"Oh, hi, Bobby," she turned towards him as he peddled slowly beside her while she walked.

"Sorry 'bout the thing on the playground today," he mumbled, his face turning the brightest shade of red which only made his freckles more prominent.

A quiet *yeah* was her only response.

Feeling even more uncomfortable, Bobby blundered ahead.

"Nobody should say anything like that about someone else's Dad," he blurted.

When there was no response, he continued.

"Ain't none of my business though. Just wanted you to know I didn't think it was right."

Willow turned to study Bobby's face, with his dark blonde hair combed to one side and his hazel eyes catching the sun's rays to lend a particular glint to them. Bobby was a good person, she was sure of that. She'd seen him in Sunday School at church the past few weeks. His mother was dead. Someone told her that his mom had been really sick and he had to help care for his little brother and sister. He was a pretty good student and understood arithmetic really well. She'd even seen Bobby take up for one of the Jones kids...the one with the limp...when he was being bullied. And she'd heard about the dog with the broken leg he had befriended and nursed back to health. Yes, Bobby Carson was a good person.

"Thanks," Willow murmured.

Bobby stood to pedal harder on his bicycle.

"See ya," he said over his shoulder.

Willow raised her hand in response and watched as Connie Brown tried to halt Bobby on his bicycle ride home. Anger crept inside Willow as she watched. Was there anything Connie Brown didn't have? How could one person get everything they ever wanted or asked for?

Up ahead was the corner where Willow would turn onto her road, the one where she and her mother lived. Children from only one other family lived beyond their house. Willow hurried to catch up with those children for the remainder of the walk. They belonged to Jedediah and Rachel Jones. Seven children in that family. Two older boys who were always getting into trouble at school; then a girl who was quiet followed in age by another boy, the one who walked with a limp. A second girl was next, followed by another boy and finally a tiny little girl. Willow knew there were times these children had no lunch at all so she was grateful for whatever was in her own brown sack at lunch time. The two older Jones boys looked healthy enough, but the little girl had a sunken look around her eyes and Willow was sure she was hungry. Willow thought her own mother was pretty good at stretching food to make meals. She knew how to fry pumpkin blossoms to make great sandwiches and quite often they had meatless meals when there was a lot of garden produce. Willow said goodbye to the Jones family and started up the dirt driveway to the brick and tar paper covered house she called home.

Eve Evans wiped perspiration from her forehead. This was Monday and that meant laundry day. She had been up early, before Willow was ever out of bed, wringing laundry through the old washing machine wringer and carrying the wet laundry from the basement out to the lines. Good day for drying. She observed there wouldn't be that many more times for hanging clothes on the line to dry. Wispy clouds predicted cooler weather and the sky was more gray than blue these days.

That meant winter was on its way and Eve hated drying clothes in the basement or all over the house. It also made it more difficult for her to get laundry finished for the Peterson family and Mrs. Peterson was very particular about how her laundry was done. Had even scolded Eve on occasion about a wrinkle in one of Mr. Peterson's white shirts. But Eve needed the income so she graciously offered to re-do the shirt and kept Mrs. Peterson as a good customer.

Eve guessed she should be grateful for the chance to earn a little bit of money. Her heart ached when she thought of winter coming on with Willow being in need of a winter coat and a new pair of shoes and what of Christmas? Tears came to Eve's eyes. She shouldn't feel sorry for herself. Others in the neighborhood were struggling as well. First the Great Depression and now WWII and rationing with the war dragging on.

Once again she wiped tears from her eyes and gave herself a good lecture. After all, the house itself was free and clear. That alone made her better off than some. All she had to do was to pay the electric bill and buy groceries. The coal bin needed filling, but she could put that off a bit if the weather held. She was a hard worker. The garden had done well and Eve spent many long hours planting and picking and harvesting and canning. Victory Gardens were all the rage with the war making such an impact on the lives of citizens. Gardening in this community, however, was a way of life not totally affected by the war. And now the last of the winter squash were in the basement. Potatoes had been dug…both Irish and sweet potatoes. Seed had been set aside for next spring's planting. Chickens resided in the hen house and eggs needed to be gathered every day. And Bossie, the cow, waited to be milked each morning. Yes, Eve Evans was indeed fortunate.

And then there was Willow. What a blessing the child was! Always helpful and seemingly content with their meager existence. Willow's hair was a mass of brown curls just like her father's had been. And her eyes sparkled just like his, so much so that Eve was lost in them just as she had been in his. For an instant, Eve's body reacted to the thought of Chuck Evans.

The rickety old truck was rumbling up the driveway and Eve's heart leaped. Chuck threw the clutch into neutral, the truck lunged and sputtered as he turned off the key and jumped from the cab only to grab her, lift her up and twirl her around before he kissed her waiting lips.

"Hey, babe," he smiled.

"What are you doing home at this time of day?" she asked, trying desperately to regain her breath.

"It's barely time for lunch."

He grabbed her around the waist as they walked towards the house.

"A machine broke down and old man Fitzgerald shut the place down for the afternoon. Didn't have a part to fix it. Dad probably won't like that decision."

"But you won't get paid for this afternoon."

"Nope. But I did make a little money today."

He dug in his pants pocket and produced two quarters and deposited them in her hand.

"Gave Ben and Harry a ride home."

"But they can't afford to pay you. You shouldn't have taken their money."

"Well, it's not the first time I've given them rides so I thought it was okay."

"So what are you gonna do on an afternoon off?" she asked.

"I'm gonna see if I can repair that back fence that's in need of fixin'. Or maybe work on the truck. It needs some attention. But first..."

At that point he picked her up and carried her to the bedroom, kissing her all the while she was squealing with delight. He lay on his side studying her face.

"Eve," he said seriously, "wanting you is just like breathing for me."

She stroked his cheek and ran her fingers through his mass of curly hair.

"I know," she whispered. "I feel the same way."

Her hand went absently to her lips with the memory.

A gust of wind pulling at the sheet she was folding brought her back to reality. Quickly finishing the task of taking down the laundry, she heaved the heavy clothesbasket into her arms as tired muscles carried it up the back stairs into the kitchen. She had just finished sprinkling the clothes and repacking them into the basket for ironing the following day when she heard the back screen door open and close. Willow was home.

Chapter Two

"What part in the Christmas play do you want, Willow?" Alice was excited as the girls made their way to school.

It was Friday and Miss Tyler had designated this day as the day parts for the Christmas play would be assigned.

"I don't know," Willow tried to sound disinterested.

Secretly she pictured herself as the fairy princess in the play. She had seen the description of the costume and her eyes glistened at the prospect. A long pink dress with sparkles on it and a silver crown for her hair and a silver scepter in her hand. She was just beginning to see herself taking a bow in front of an admiring audience and could almost hear the applause beginning when her thoughts were interrupted by the whirr of bicycle wheels. Mud from a nearby puddle flew over her shoes and socks and the bottom of her dress and worst of all, on the arithmetic homework assignment which had fallen out of the book on impact.

Alice flew into a rage and ran after Bucky Wilson who by the time Willow bent to pick up the soiled paper, was laughing as he spun his bicycle through other puddles, splattering dirt and muddy water over other unsuspecting victims.

Willow picked up the soggy assignment. Daily lessons were written out on a newsprint kind of paper, a cheaper version of tablet. Slick white paper was reserved for special things like mid-semester tests and the like. But, unfortunately, the newsprint type paper did not hold up well in water…or mud.

By the time Alice retreated from her chase and came wheezing back to Willow, the arithmetic assignment was one gigantic blob in Willow's hand.

Willow's face was still in a state of shock.

"Whatever are you gonna do, Willow?"

A numbed Willow turned slowly and then the tears came.

"I don't know," Willow sobbed.

"I'll tell Miss Tyler what happened," Alice offered. "I think she'll believe me."

"It's not about that," Willow informed. "It's about all the time I spent on it and I don't know if I can do it over again. I really hate 'rithmetic."

"Oh, look out, Willow," Alice gasped, "here he comes again."

The girls looked up to see Bucky Wilson barreling back towards them for an extra dose of mischief. This time the girls were ready and flew into action. As if orchestrated by some professional choreographer, Willow's foot moved forward and caught the wheel of the bike at the same time Alice gave a push against Bucky's shoulder. It was just enough to catch him off balance and he hit the ground with a thud, deposing him from his arrogant seat and deflating his ego from its previous height. Bucky recovered quickly; but before he could retaliate, another bicycle loomed into sight and Bobby Carson placed himself and his bicycle between Bucky and the girls. Bucky's fist came down hard on Bobby's face and he kicked the front fender of Bobby's bike so hard, he bent the fender cover. Apparently feeling as if his outburst of temper had been vindicated, he righted his bicycle and sped off.

Willow was the first to reach him.

"Oh, Bobby, your face! It's bleeding."

She grabbed a clean handkerchief from her pocket and began wiping as he slowly resisted. He was more interested in the damage to the bike.

"It's okay," he murmured as he gently brushed her hand away and hastily looked around to see if anyone was observing.

Then he busied himself straightening and pulling at the fender metal until he had pulled it free from the tire. Seemingly too embarrassed to linger any longer, he gave a push to the bike; and throwing his leg over the cross bar, sped away on his way to school.

"Oh, Bobby," Willow called after him as she stooped to pick up papers Bobby had dropped from his pocket. But he was already too far to hear.

"You can return them to him at school," Alice suggested. "What is it?"

Willow opened the muddy papers.

"It's the arithmetic homework," she sighed.

Miss Tyler listened to the explanation. Two arithmetic papers muddy and wet. Accounts of the incident were pretty compatible...at least the ones from Alice, Willow and Bobby. There was no doubt in Miss Tyler's mind that Bucky Wilson was probably responsible for the incident. But homework assignments were required. That meant recess would be sacrificed and spent duplicating the arithmetic assignment. However, Miss Tyler had a meeting to attend and smiled as she knew for certain that Bobby was going to help Willow with the arithmetic paper. Bucky was always in trouble and would be spending recess with the principal as he frequently did.

Bobby felt a pang of sympathy when he observed the mud splatters on Willow's dress and she felt equal sympathy when she saw the red scrape on Bobby's cheek.

But this was Friday and no matter if there were scratched faces or muddy dresses, the selection of the parts for the Christmas play were to take place. Willow's tummy danced wildly. If only she could be the princess in the Christmas play, things would be wonderful. Again, visions of Willow taking bows before parents and friends and seeing Mother sitting in the audience being proud of her filled her head. Excitement pounded in her body as Miss Tyler instructed all the students to put away their books and pencils for the day. She assured the students that everyone would have a part whether it be singing in the chorus or speaking or helping with the stage crew. Every part would be important and no one would be left out.

With that announcement, students began whispering excitedly among themselves. In the fray, Connie Brown remarked to the girl next to her.

"Maybe Willow can be a tree. After all, her name *is* a tree. Who names their child after a tree?"

Several students in close proximity to Connie's remarks giggled and Miss Tyler called for order in the classroom. Tears stung at Willow's eyes, but she fought them; and an understanding look from Alice bolstered her to swallow and kept the moisture from materializing.

It was a silent walk home. Willow refused to give in to the feelings of disappointment that welled up inside her by trying to swallow the lump that had formed in her throat. She was doing some strong talking to herself when Alice's words overcame them

"It's okay, Willow," she encouraged. "Like Miss Tyler said we'd all get parts and we have. I kinda wanted to be Mary, but being a shepherd is okay with me. I'm glad you got the part instead of someone else. And Joe will do a good job with the part of the father in the play."

Here she paused to giggle.

"Although I don't think he's all that excited about Connie getting the part of the mother."

"I didn't know you wanted to be Mary. I think you'd make a great one."

"Yeah I thought I might, but when I saw you were getting the part, I was okay with that."

"Guess you know that's not the part I wanted," Willow said quietly.

"What part did you want?"

"It's not important now," Willow refused to confess. "I'm just happy that Connie didn't get the part of the princess."

"You wanted to be the princess?" Alice gasped.

Willow blushed at the thought she'd let her secret be discovered.

"Oh, just for a split second I thought it might be fun, but I don't think the costume would fit me anyway; and besides that, there are a lot of lines to learn."

"You will make a good Mary. And Bobby will make a good Joseph."

By this time, the girls were approaching Alice's house and they bid their goodbyes for the weekend. Willow hurried to catch up with the Jones family. Jane, the smallest of the family, seemed to be paler than ever. She lagged behind the rest of the family and Willow lagged with her, walking slowly enough so the little one could keep up the pace. It gave Willow great peace to lose herself in giving to someone else. She rattled on about the events of the day and finally brought a smile to the little girl's face. By the time they reached the Evans' driveway, Jane was sharing as well.

World War II was raging in Europe. Willow really knew very little about it. For her, it meant rationing, doing without certain items that were limited. Mother said those things were needed to support the troops and the war effort. In that way, she possibly felt like she was a small part of the war; but by in large, it was something that was happening far away from Illinois.

Former classmate Mary Louise's mother had moved their family to Michigan in order to work in a factory there. Lots of women were doing jobs previously thought to be jobs only men could do. Pearl Harbor had been bombed earlier in the month. A horrific tragedy. She'd overheard adults speak of that. And she knew Mother's younger brother, Uncle Zach, was somewhere in the thick of things and hadn't been heard from for a long time. Willow's life was more about going to school, studying hard and playing with friends.

Chapter Three

Stairs creaked as Eve Evans made her way up the steps to the attic. A musty smell greeted her as she unlatched the door. Reaching for the chain on the overhead single bulb which shed little light upon the contents of the room, she let a sigh escape from her mouth. Spread before her were an assortment of treasures that represented her life. She tried to concentrate on her reason for being there…looking for some fabric she thought she remembered being tucked away somewhere; but she was distracted by an old trunk crouching in one corner. Dust testifying to the length of time it had been left undisturbed, fell to the floor as she raised the lid. Dried roses tied with pink ribbons caught her attention and she picked them up and put them to her nose as if there would still be fragrance there. Closing her eyes, she envisioned the little country church and the pink dress trimmed with lace she wore on her wedding day. But foremost in her mind's eyes was the face that waited for her at the front of the church. Chuck Evans. Love of her life. She blushed as she remembered the shock of brown curls that cascaded over his forehead, the squareness of his shoulders on his lanky body, the look of love in his eyes.

She'd always been attracted to him although from afar; and when he approached her and asked her to go to a movie with him, her heart beat uncontrollably. She had been with friends who pushed her back into reality to accept his offer. Such excitement she had never felt before. And the evening had been great. First, the fun of selecting just the right skirt and blouse to wear. Wearing just a bit too much makeup. Mother's questioning glance. Then hearing Chuck's old truck coming for her. A wonderful movie which she could not even recall, but it had been wonderful. Then a walk to the soda shop where they sat and talked over chocolate sodas. After returning to her home, they had continued their talk to the sound of the squeaking porch swing on her parents' front porch.

Chuck Evans was a superstar, a football player in high school. After high school, he had attended state college for one year, but finances were limited so he went to work in his father's business and that was the end of college. They married just as soon as Eve was graduated from high school and Willow was born one year to the day after their wedding. Chuck was a great father and Eve did not recall even one day they weren't head over heels in love with each other. Yes, it had been a perfect union and a perfect little girl was the result of that love.

Eve tenderly placed the roses back in the trunk and picked up the photo album. Tears came to her eyes as the pages turned in her trembling fingers. Eve and Chuck at the church picnic. Both of them on their wedding day. So happy. Chuck and Eve camping in the old tent…

"Hey, Evie Joanne, hurry up!" Chuck shouted over his shoulder as he hoisted a box into the back of the pickup.

He always called her by her two names when he was teasing with her or being tender. He surveyed the bed of the truck. Sleeping bags, blankets, cooking utensils, tent and pegs, small camp stove, lanterns. It was all there. Everything they would need for a weekend campout. Everything that is except his beloved bride. The mere thought of her sent darting aches across his loins. He never tired of looking at her or talking to her and he absolutely adored the little giggle she uttered when she was loving him.

"I'm coming," she replied, taking time to brush her hair back from her face. She stopped to adjust the headband she used to hold her taffy colored hair in place and then lifted the cooler once again. He took it from her, taking time to notice how she looked in rolled up jeans and the checkered blouse tied up at the waist.

A few minutes later they were on their way down the two lane road, jostling back and forth as the truck exceeded its capabilities in speed. He looked at her out of the corner of his eye.

"You are so beautiful," he complimented, gently putting his hand on her leg.

"Silly," she giggled. "Here I am in faded jeans and an old shirt and you think I'm beautiful?"

He removed his hand to take control of the steering wheel. Morning sun glistened across her face, bringing a sparkling look to her blue eyes; and a breeze playing inside the open window messed playfully with her hair.

"You are beautiful. I still can't believe you are mine. I must be the luckiest guy in the world."

"I feel the same way," she said softly.

They laughed.

"Well, not that you're the luckiest, but that I am. I hope you'll feel that way when we celebrate our 50th anniversary. After all, two months is hardly a test of marital happiness."

"Honey, if I was any happier than I am now, I don't know what I'd do."

She glanced his way and studied the strong jaw line and the shock of brown curly hair which tumbled so freely over his forehead. Much like him, she thought. Always a bit of a rebel. The shape of his firm shoulders and forearms sent little thrills throughout her body. It was so easy to love Chuck Evans.

"How long before we get there?" she asked.

"My, aren't you the impatient one?"

She sighed.

"You know I've never been camping before."

"Good," he replied with a menacing grin. "You won't know if things are going well or not."

He paused.

"No bathroom, you know."

"You're kidding!"

He chuckled. He loved her childlike innocence and how easily he could use it to tease her.

"If you're going to be a real camper," he continued the ruse, "you're going to have to learn to rough it."

"But no bathroom!" she pouted.

"Well, there is one of sorts, but you'll have to rid it of the squirrels and raccoons that have taken up residence there and you'll have to be brave enough to chase them out."

Her eyes widened in disbelief.

"And you did remember to bring the barbeque, didn't you?"

She gasped.

"You told me fried chicken, didn't you? Yes, I'm quite sure that was your request. It was fried chicken. I don't think I'm mistaken."

Chuck gave vent to the laughter he'd been containing. Eve attempted to regain her composure.

"That's exactly what I told you, honey. Just teasing."

She scooted over next to him and he extended his arm around her while she rested her head on his shoulder. The surge within her body grew stronger each time they were together. He responded as well, rubbing her arm with his right hand, driving with his left. He turned enough to kiss the top of her head.

"Umm," he murmured. "I do love you, Evie Joanne."

"Oh, yes," she responded. "You are the one and only man of my dreams."

They rode in silence for a while. Then she sat up straight.

"Really! Raccoons in the bathroom!"

Chuck roared with laughter. Eve made his heart light.

Eve smiled as she continued through the memories from the photo album. Their first Christmas. Chuck with his hands around Eve's expanding body when she was pregnant with Willow. Chuck and Eve with baby Willow. Willow's first Christmas. Willow's first attempt at walking. Willow with Grandma and Grandpa Evans. Eve with Willow and Eve's parents, George and Blanche Cain. Chuck and three of his oldest buddies together. Hank Robertson, Jerry Wells and Stace Grant. Well, at least Hank and Jerry were good friends. Eve studied the face of Stace Grant. She had never wanted Chuck to be friends with Stace, but he always told her Stace was an okay guy, just a little demented and then he'd laugh his robust laugh. But Eve never trusted Stace. At least not after that afternoon.

"I saw you last night, Eve."

His temper was flaring more than usual.

She nodded.

"He's not good enough for you," Stace tightened his grip on her arm.

"You're hurting me," she said, pulling her arm away from his hand.

Anger flashed in his eyes and his voice deepened.

"You're my girl," he insisted.

"A few dates does not make me your girl," she shot back, each word driving a bullet into his pride.

"I thought we had something goin'. You and me…Come on, Eve. I'm sorry if I hurt your arm. I didn't mean to."

Eve did not relent.

"I do not wish to see you anymore. Not as boyfriend and girlfriend. I never promised you anything. Now I'm gonna walk away from here and I do not wish you to follow me."

She turned cautiously, keeping in mind that Stace had a terrible temper. There had been incidents with other guys and fist fights, but he had always treated her with care. That is, up until now."

"You'll regret this, Eve. You'll come crawling back to me, you hear? And that jerk you seem so infatuated with will regret it, too. You hear me, Eve? Do you hear me?"

He was shouting, but she continued to walk away from him as he scuffed the dirt with his shoe in disgust. Who needed Eve Cain anyway? She'd regret ever ditching him. And so would Chuck Evans. He'd see to that.

Eve shuddered. That had been so long ago she had all but forgotten it, but the images in the photo brought back the emotion. Stace had not been accepted into the army because of an injury he sustained in a knife fight. He had married Julie, a girl from their graduating class and stayed in the area, but Eve rarely saw him; and when she did, she felt nothing but uneasiness. But he was in the picture album and had seemed to be friendly with Chuck.

She continued reminiscing through the photograph album. Chuck and Eve on their sixth wedding anniversary. Chuck and her brother Zach in their army uniforms right before they were to ship out. Eve ran a sensitive finger over their faces in the photos perhaps in an effort to draw some degree of comfort. It was there the photos stopped and the tears continued.

Ignoring other significant items in the trunk, Eve closed the lid once more as if her body could not endure any more memories…memories too painful to remember, too precious to forget.

Rummaging through two boxes finally revealed what Eve was looking for…a piece of unused cloth folded and begging to be used. This indeed would make Willow a fine new dress for Christmas. Gifts would be pretty scare this year…again. As Eve moved to stand, still holding the piece of fabric close to her, she noticed an old gray coat hanging on a hook. Taking it from its resting place on the brown peg, Eve evaluated its worthiness and surmised it could be used. Willow needed a new coat and a creative Eve saw possibilities. She could remodel it she thought into a serviceable coat to protect Willow against the winter cold. Clutching the prizes she'd found, she descended the stairs, visions of doing something special for Willow whirling in her head. But she would have to hurry. Time was short and she needed to work while Willow was at school in order for the gifts to be a surprise on Christmas morning. The door closed and with it the memories so dear to Eve's heart.

"Willow, can you deliver these things to your grandparents on your way to school?"

"Sure," Willow answered as she pulled on the red rubber boots to cover her shoes. Rainy days and rubber boots always went together. Ugh!

Later she would remove them in the school hallway. They were a pain because invariably the shoes came off with the rubber boots and she would have to balance on one foot while pulling the trapped shoes from their confinement, trying hard not to put her sock foot down on the cold and often wet floor and trying to conceal the hole she knew existed in the toe of her stocking. But the rubber boots helped to keep the rain and snow from penetrating the shoes with the holes in their soles.

Willow liked the walk to school. Along the way, she might see women shaking rugs and dust mops out their front doors or perhaps sweeping off their front porches; or old Mr. Clanton pruning his rose bushes or scooping snow in season or raking leaves in the fall of the year; or see women hanging clothes on the outdoor lines on Monday mornings. Friendly dogs often wagged their tails as they heard her approach. All would stop to wave at Willow as she went by. She could call them all by name and knew their families and they knew her. She could go to any of these houses if she was hurt or needed help in any way. It was a true neighborhood where people cared about their neighbors. It was a very comfortable place to be.

With the package to be dropped off at Grandma Cain's house and her arithmetic book under one arm and the brown paper lunch bag in the other, Willow set out on her morning trek. Grandma and Grandpa Cain lived in a two story white frame house on Willow's way to school. Gingerbread trimmed the eaves while dark green paint edged the doors and windows. Immaculately trimmed hedges framed the perimeter of the yard and a concrete sidewalk led to the front door. A vineyard in the backyard with rows and rows of grape arbors stretched from one side to the other. Willow and Eve had harvested those in the fall of the year both for selling and making juice and jelly. Spring and summer months produced a yard filled with the aroma of flowers of all kinds and colors. Now berries on holly bushes near the front entrance were beginning to turn from green to red in preparation for the upcoming winter season.

"Land sakes, Willow, come on in out of this wet, child," Grandma Cain met her at the door.

"Can't stay, Grandma," Willow replied. "I'm on my way to school."

"Well, stop by after school. I'll have a cup o' tea ready for you."

By the time Willow returned from school, Grandma Cain was busy starting soup for supper and had the tea ready as she'd promised. Willow didn't really care that much for tea, but she knew it was important to her grandmother. Besides that, the tea was almost assuredly accompanied by one of Grandma's oatmeal cookies.

As Grandpa Cain entered the room, Grandma got up from her chair at the table.

"Glad you're here, George," she said. "Here's a box that needs to go to the basement."

"Now, Blanche," Grandpa said with a twinkle in his eye and a wink towards Willow, "I know you jest been waitin' for me to come by so I could do this chore."

"Oh, go on with you," Blanche Cain dismissed him.

"Can I go, too, Grandpa?"

"Sure thing, little one," Grandpa said as he picked up the box and hoisted it to his shoulder.

"What you got in here, Blanche? Heavier than two blocks of ice, it is," George groaned, putting on an extra bit of drama for his young granddaughter.

Then he chuckled as he heard his wife give an audible sigh at his antics.

Following Grandpa down the wooden stairs to the basement, Willow perused the shelves while Grandpa found a spot for the cardboard box. A red heart-shaped box caught her imagination.

"What's this, Grandpa?" Willow asked, fingering a valentine box.

Grandpa Cain glanced at the heart shaped cardboard.

"Harumph," he grunted. "A young man gave it to your Mom. Glad she didn't end up with him. He was no good."

"Not like my Dad."

"No, not at all like your Dad."

Willow smiled, content in the fact that Dad had been a good choice in Grandpa's eyes and continued exploring the basement.

"How about this, Grandpa?" she asked, pulling a small wooden box from a shelf.

Grandpa took the box and wiped the dust from the top.

"This, I believe," he started," is a wooden box that belonged to your Mother. I made it for her myself when she was about your age. She used to keep her most valuable possessions in there," he added with a bit of intrigue.

Willow was quick to see an opportunity.

"Could we clean it up, Grandpa?"

"Whatever for?"

But Willow had plans.

"I want to clean it up and make it pretty for Mother for Christmas."

"Well, I guess we could do that." Grandpa thought as he stroked the days' growth of whiskers on his chin. "It'll need some sanding and refinishing, but we could do that."

And so it was that Willow and Grandpa Cain set about refinishing the wooden box on Thursdays after school. Near its completion, she had the idea of painting some flowers on the lid. Grandpa found some paint and helped her as she mixed the colors and carefully applied them to the wood. With a stretch to relieve the tension in her shoulders and a survey of her work, she allowed a smile to cross her face. And with a glance at Grandpa's approving expression, she laid down the brush with a great deal of satisfaction. It was indeed going to be a great gift!

Scenes from the Christmas play were really rough. Seasonal colds and coughs played havoc with Miss Tyler's fifth graders. Scenery, constructed from limited available materials, was fragile and quite often was in need of repair. Indeed, *Christmas Memories* was in trouble from its inception.

But nothing would compare to the night of the performance. With parents and friends tightly packed into the folding chairs carried in for the occasion at the small schoolhouse, excitement ran rampant among the students. Miss Tyler welcomed everyone, the lights went down and a hush fell over the audience as students presented the first part of the Christmas program. Everything went well until one of the trees lost his vision through the holes in his costume and became disoriented and started roaming the stage. The fairy princess staggered under the weight of her costume and hurled the magic wand right into laps of people seated in the first row of the audience. No amount of magic could repair that damage although Connie Brown, in one grand effort to save the show, began to vary from the script. This confused everyone else...those less talented actors than Ms. Brown...to the point that no one knew where the individual lines were supposed to be said and finally Miss Tyler called for the curtains (drapes from Mrs. Miller's living room) to be drawn.

The second half of the show which focused on the birth of Christ was no better. The angel started her lines with *And behold*...but her halo kept slipping and she tried pushing it back with one hand while repeating the same line over and over again. One of the supposedly terrified shepherds, losing his composure, thought it was funny and began to snicker. It ran through those on stage like a bad virus until all the shepherds were shaking with laughter. That set off the next series of disasters with a piece of the scenery falling over, one of the wise men sneezing and dropping the gift intended for the baby Jesus and culminated with the choir's out of tune rendition of *Silent Night*. In fact, Willow herself, playing a very demure Mary holding her doll representing the baby Jesus, would have completely collapsed had it not been for Bobby Carson, a very much in control Joseph, placing a hand firmly on her shoulder.

But bows were taken, the audience gave a rousing round of applause and a disheveled Miss Tyler breathed a sigh of relief as she smiled and congratulated each individual student. It certainly would be a Christmas program not easily forgotten.

Only two days of school remained after the night of Miss Tyler's fifth grade Christmas program. There was less schoolwork to be accomplished. Miss Tyler read Christmas stories to the class and there was an art project and the making of Christmas cards. And best of all, there was no arithmetic.

With the craft from Miss Tyler's fifth grade class tucked inside her coat, Willow started the walk home. Excitement about the upcoming holiday was at an all-time high. Alice and Willow giggled and speculated about what Santa would leave under the tree. Both girls were convinced that Santa Claus didn't really exist, but the concept still gave them a feeling of awe. It in no way less dampened the thought of Christmas lights and gifts and goodies. With a hasty goodbye and the promise they would see each other at the church Christmas program rehearsal on Saturday, the girls parted ways.

Willow's heart was light. No school for almost two whole weeks! She would miss seeing friends and Miss Tyler, but the idea of no arithmetic sent little shivers of pleasure throughout her body. She ran to catch up with little Jane Jones. As she noticed the holes in the gloves Jane wore, saw the shoe being held together with a piece of twine tied around it and the tears in the tiny girl's eyes, Willow indeed felt fortunate and hardly felt the hole in the sole of her own shoe or noticed the patches in her own clothing. She stood for some time at the end of the drive way watching after the Jones children as they trudged towards their home and wondered what their evening would be. Thoughts of gifts that might be under the Evans' Christmas tree gave way to what she imagined would be lacking in the Jones' household. Sadness came over her as she walked slowly up the dirt driveway into Eve Evan's warm kitchen.

"Willow," Eve greeted. "School's out for Christmas break. Shouldn't you be happy about that?"

"Oh, I am happy about that alright," Willow mustered a smile as she hugged mother.

Eve looked up from her work and studied her young daughter's serious look.

"Then why the long face?"

"It's Jane Jones. Well, the whole Jones family. I don't think they have much to eat."

Eve smoothed the mending she was working on and folded it neatly to lay it aside before she answered.

"Willow, no one has much right now. We've talked about that. The war and all, you know."

Eve made conscious efforts to talk as little about the war as possible without minimizing its importance. Most people in their community were poor anyway so the war probably had less impact on them than the more affluent areas. Scraping to get by during the war wasn't that different from scraping to get by before the war.

"I know that, Mom, but we have something to eat. I'm not sure they do. I don't think any of the kids ever have lunch."

"Well, do you think there's something we can do?" Eve wisely asked.

"I'll think about it," Willow said wistfully.

"What's that bulge in your coat, Willow?"

"Oh," she stammered. "Just something from school."

Eve turned away and smiled.

"It's Christmastime," she said. "A time for secrets and surprises. You run upstairs now and change into your play clothes."

She listened as Willow scampered up the stairs.

"And don't forget to hang up your dress," she called after her.

Chores came first. Playing and fun things after that, but chores always first. Without being reminded, Willow removed the glass butter churn from the pantry shelf and took the bowl of cream which had been skimmed from the crocks of milk from its place in the icebox. Remembering to close the icebox door to keep the block of ice from melting so quickly, she poured the contents of the bowl into the glass base of the churn and set up her work space on the kitchen steps. Screwing on the top that held the wooden paddles, she commenced to turn the handle around and around blending the cream until it became a smooth mixture.

Mother enjoyed having Willow's company in the sunny kitchen and listened carefully as Willow shared all that had happened during the school day. She realized that someday Willow might not be as open as she was at this age so Eve listened intently as she squeezed the cloth bag filled with a cooked cream mixture which was being formed into cottage cheese.

Mother's homemade cottage cheese was a real treat and it wasn't often made. Eve continued to work at the kitchen sink, keeping an eye on the difficulty of the turn of the crank. At just the right time she relieved Willow of the chore and separated the formed butter from the liquid. Eve continued to work the yellow ball with a short wooden paddle until it was free of all the excess liquid. Cool glasses of buttermilk tasted real good with leftover cornbread.

With chores behind her, Willow was more than ready for the traditional Christmas activities. Sure enough flour and sugar purchased with ration stamps and carefully stored away for the occasion were on the kitchen table along with eggs and butter and vanilla. It was Christmas cookie baking time, a favorite activity for Willow at the holidays. She stirred and measured and mixed and rolled out the dough under Mother's watchful eye. Tin cookie cutters in shapes of a bell, a star, a candy cane and a

Santa Clause cut into the rolled out dough and the wonderful cookie dough shapes were carefully transported to the cookie sheet for baking. After removal from the oven, they were transferred to a clean muslin dishtowel for cooling. A small amount of frosting was prepared for the decorating. Any more would have been wasteful. Willow chose blue for the stars and yellow for the bells and bright red for the candy canes and Santas. It was a superb afternoon with delicious smells in Mama's kitchen.

"Mama," Willow said thoughtfully, "don't we have some vegetables we could spare?"

Eve was pretty sure where Willow was headed with that statement.

"I suppose," she said with pride in her small daughter, realizing what was about to take place.

"I walked home with the Jones children. Mother, I think they don't have enough to eat. Maybe we could share with the Jones family.

"What a thoughtful thing to suggest," she replied.

"Well, it's kinda like Grandma Bessie says, *'Tis more blessed to give than to receive.*

Tears came to Eve's eyes as her heart swelled with pride at Willow's generosity.

"I believe Grandma Bessie has the right idea. Let's get these dishes cleaned up and see what we can do."

After dishes, Eve went to the large storage box of outgrown clothing and selected some outgrown or not used articles that perhaps the Jones family could use.

Taking a muslin grain bag with them, they went to the cellar where they placed white potatoes, sweet potatoes, turnips, winter squash and walnuts and apples into the sack. Having thought the whole thing through, Willow surmised the blue and white print on the grain bag might also be of help if Mrs. Jones knew how to sew.

Willow even decided to part with an old doll she seldom played with anymore and a jump rope and a ball and jacks. Sorting through her marble collection, she selected a dozen or so she thought she could do without. These were all placed in a bag with the other items for the Jones family.

Saturday morning was another special time, a day for making chocolate fudge. Tricky job, this fudge making. Ingredients must be carefully measured, cooked for just the right amount of time. Mother checked the temperature of the boiling mixture several times by dropping a small amount in a cup of cold water. When it formed into just the right ball, it was time to remove it from the stove, add the vanilla and butter and wait for it to cool a bit before starting the process of beating. Willow's arms hurt and her hands ached but she continued to beat the sweet mixture, realizing the end product would be worth the effort. Not cooking the mixture just the right time or beating just the right amount of time could result in candy that would either turn to sugar or not set up properly. And its ingredients were so rationed that one could not afford to make a mistake. Just when Willow thought her arms could not make another rotation with the big wooden spoon, mother took over and it wasn't long until the brown confection was poured into a waiting pan.

While it was setting and cooling, Willow and Eve donned their winter coats and started off towards the Jones' house with the bag of food and clothing as well as a couple dozen eggs and fresh milk. As they approached the door, Eve wondered if the meager bag of food would make much difference against the problems of this dilapidated house. Their knock on the door was met by a fragile looking woman. Several of the younger children crowded behind their mother, looking out to see who had come to the door on this winter day.

Eve let Willow speak.

"Hello, Mrs. Jones," she said. "My Mom and I wanted to share some things with you for Christmas."

The hollow-eyed woman just stared in return. Then, rubbing her hand nervously across her hair which had pulled itself loose from its bun and wiping her hands on a well-used apron, she stammered, "Won't you come in?"

Willow and Eve stepped inside the small room which contained a kitchen area at one end and a heating stove putting out very little heat situated to one side of the room. Two chairs were placed close to the stove. An unshaven Mr. Jones sat in one of the chairs with a blanket across his lap. Laundry was strung across one end of the room to dry. Blankets which the children obviously had pulled around themselves to keep warm lay on the bare floor. Two doors opened into the room and Eve thought they were probably bedrooms, unheated rooms.

Becoming aware of their meager surroundings, Mrs. Jones stammered, "You'll have to excuse the house. We all been sick."

Now Willow knew that wasn't true. The Jones children had been in school every day for the past two weeks or so.

"We aren't staying," Eve tried to put Mrs. Jones at ease.

"Willow and I had a little extra food and some things Willow has outgrown and thought perhaps, well, with the children and all and Christmas coming up, that perhaps you could use it."

"We don't take charity."

It was the first time Mr. Jones had acknowledged them.

Willow, in all her innocence, moved closer to him. Eve's first instinct was to hold her back, but made no move to do so. Willow struggled with the weight of the bag as she laid it at Mr. Jones' feet.

"It ain't charity, Mr. Jones. It's Merry Christmas."

The man's countenance softened, but Willow didn't stay around to notice. She and Eve left the house with one final *Merry Christmas* and an invitation to the church Christmas program on Sunday evening. They paused on the broken down porch for a few moments after the door closed behind them. Inside they heard the squeals of the children as they found the treasures of the apples and nuts and other goodies in the blue and white bag.

By the time they returned to the house, the fudge was set so it was scored, cut and stored just in time to set off for rehearsal of Sunday's Christmas program at church. Willow would have liked to have taken the car to church. But gas was another thing that was rationed so Eve and Willow bundled themselves up in gloves and scarves and walked the distance to the little brick church where they met with other mothers and children.

The church building was cold. No heating fuel would be wasted on a Saturday rehearsal when church was within walking distance. Sunday was the only day heat would be in the building. It would be a quick rehearsal with children keeping their coats on. Children sat in rows with others from each individual Sunday School class. Mrs. Roberts stood before them and explained that as each person's name was called, they should come to the platform and *speak their pieces* and then return to their seats. Willow was nervous until it was her turn; and when she heard her name announced, she made her way out of the row of students and onto the platform and spoke her practiced recitation loud and clear. Then she could relax and listen to others. Willow knew that Alice and Bobby would do well with their recitations but she grew impatient with those who had not mastered their memorization and required prompting from their Sunday School teachers.

Eve and Willow walked back home in the chill of the clear night. Willow's hand felt secure in her mother's hand. Besides, Mama's hand was warm on this cold evening. A good feeling filled her heart. Other children were walking with their parents as well. An occasional light in a house window lit up the night. They wouldn't be lit for long. The war had put an end to light on dark nights. They were called blackouts, practiced throughout America as a precaution against possible invasion. A light snow began to fall and the sky was dotted with stars.

As Willow enjoyed the gently falling snow, Eve was remembering another chilly winter evening, one in which Chuck's arm had been securely wrapped around her, giving her comfort and protection. She thought she could still hear the laughter and singing and the gentle jingling sounds of bells on the horses' collars as they pulled a sleigh over the white snow. There was always something magical about the sound of sleigh bells. How long ago had that taken place? Sometimes it seemed like an eon ago and sometimes it felt like yesterday. But the image of Eve and Chuck snuggling together in perfect happiness stayed with Eve all the way home.

Grandpa George delivered an evergreen tree two days prior so now was the time to decorate. Willow was counting the days. This was Saturday, tomorrow was church in the morning and the church Christmas program tomorrow night...this year on Christmas Eve. Now was the perfect time to adorn the tree with the small string of lights and the few ornaments from the big metal box kept in the attic. Willow cut pictures from last year's Christmas cards and strung them to hang on the branches so bare of glass ornaments. A star topped the tree and then silver icicles draped over the tips of the branches completed the picture as Willow and Eve stood back to observe their handiwork. Hot cocoa was a special treat and Willow was allowed to stay up longer than usual.

Willow and Alice could hardly sit through Reverend Morgan's sermon on Sunday morning. Someone had decorated the church with greenery; and red candles in the windows and a small tree at one side of the platform completed the festive atmosphere of the season. Willow went over the lines to her recitation in her mind and wondered if she would indeed remember it for the evening. She was relieved when the last hymn was sung and the last prayer was given. Not even Willow's preparation of her Christmas gift for her mother could quench the excitement in her stomach. It was a long afternoon before Mother finally said it was time to get ready again for church.

The Sunday evening church Christmas program fared better than Miss Tyler's fifth grade extravaganza. Everyone was as clean as soap and water could manage and best clothes were put on for the occasion. People who never ever attended church services before filled the pews at this season and men from the church carried in folding chairs, borrowed for the event, to accommodate the crowd.

Willow saw Grandma Blanche and Grandpa George smiling encouragingly from their usual seats in the fifth row from the front. It was always easy to find them because they always sat in the same place every Sunday and even on special occasions. Mother sat beside them, looking as beautiful as ever. And although they didn't often attend church, the entire Jones family shuffled in and found seats near the back of the church. Willow was excited to see one of her used dresses on one of the girls. What a great feeling to know she had been part of helping someone. Lights dimmed announcing the beginning of the program. Children's recitations were first on the program and all went well with those. Their part in the program was followed by the nativity story presented by the adults.

Willow and Alice, relieved their part of the program was over, sat in awe and wonderment as they listened to the story of the shepherds and wise men and Mary and Joseph and the baby Jesus all enhanced by music from the once-a-year choir. Makeshift costumes added to the gala. When the lights came back on, Christmas cards were passed out from friends and neighbors, another way the mid-war populace could save money. Every child delighted in receiving a small brown paper bag containing an orange and several pieces of hard candy as well as a couple of chocolate drops and a candy cane. A small piece of peanut brittle was Willow's favorite. The excitement on the faces of the Jones family was unforgettable. Willow's Sunday School teacher gave each student in her class a coloring book. All who attended wished others a Merry Christmas. Even Mr. Jones seemed to have a small amount of Christmas spirit and Willow and Eve left with a good feeling in their hearts. Christmas was a great time of year.

Bright sun glistening on newly fallen snow welcomed Christmas day. Willow woke to the smells of pumpkin pie and other delicious aromas wafting from the kitchen. She stretched leisurely under the big comforter until she realized it was indeed Christmas day. That meant perhaps Santa had paid a visit. She leaped from her bed; and wrapping her flannel robe around her, she hurried down the stairs to the living room. Eve, hearing the sound of footsteps, met Willow near the tree.

"Come see what Santa has left for you," she announced proudly.

Willow fell to her knees next to the packages.

"Oh, mother," she gasped. "I didn't expect…"

She hugged her mother even before she opened the packages.

"Go ahead," Eve said quietly, "open them."

Unlike other children, Willow took her time, careful to save the string and paper. A new dress *and* a new coat. What more could she ask for? This was already a great Christmas. Eve had done a splendid job of remodeling the old gray coat she'd found hanging in the attic. She buttoned the shiny new buttons around Willow's slender frame, pleased she had such a good fit with still room to grow. There was more. A box of crayons and a new pencil and tablet. Practical but appreciated in this scarcity of war time.

"Oh, Mama," she cried. "Thank you so much. Can I wear it today?"

"Of course," Eve couldn't deny her young daughter. "Grandma Cain and Aunt Flo will want to see you in it anyway. But chores first, so hurry. They will be here soon."

Bundling against the cold, Willow went to the chicken coop to feed the hens and gather the eggs. She forked hay over to the cow and filled her watering trough with water. Chores would be done quickly today. No dawdling. No time for breakfast either. Willow hurriedly peeled the orange she had received at church last night. Such a treat. Anything fresh and out of the ordinary was a treat. That would be sufficient until Christmas dinner. Christmas dinner would come quick enough with all there was to do before time for company's arrival. Grandma and Grandpa Cain would be there and Aunt Flo, mama's sister and husband, Uncle Gage. There was a time, Willow barely remembered now, when Daddy was there on Christmas day as well as his parents, Grandma and Grandpa Evans. She hadn't seen those grandparents since shortly after Daddy died; and their faces were difficult to recall anymore. Uncle Zach had gone off to the war. He wasn't talked about much. No word had been received from him for over four months now because Willow overheard Mama and Grandma Cain talking about it in hushed tones; and a wise Willow, although curious, kept her questions to herself.

Willow quickly put on her new dress with Mama's permission for this special day and busied herself setting the table with the good china, taking special care to make sure every plate, every glass and piece of silverware were all correctly displayed on the white tablecloth with the pink and green trim. And there were cloth napkins as well. Then it was off to the kitchen to help with dinner. It would be roasted chicken today since they were raised from chicks in the spring of the year. Mother had been up early and stuffed them with sage dressing and they were roasting in the oven. Two pumpkin pies were cooling on the shelf. Willow helped peel potatoes for mashing. There would also be sweet potatoes as well as mashed potatoes, gravy, noodles, canned green beans from the garden, canned corn from the garden, freshly baked yeast rolls and best of all fresh cranberries and greens.

Aunt Flo, with a mince pie in her hands, and Uncle Gage, his arms filled with gaily wrapped presents, were the first to arrive.

"Oh, Eve," she gushed, "everything looks so festive."

"Doin' the best we can," Eve smiled, returning her sister's embrace.

Uncle Gage gave Eve a quick hug and gave Willow's cheek a slight pinch.

"My, you're getting to be quite a little lady, Willow."

As long as she could remember, Uncle Gage had used that same greeting. Willow mumbled a response as she concentrated on the armload of packages Uncle Gage was carrying.

Aunt Flo was Mother's older sister. Her slender form always looked neat and trim in her dresses with the high shoulder pads. Dark ringlets of hair swept up and held in place with two combs accented her pale skin and dark eyes. She favored Blanche Cain while Eve displayed more of their father's coloring. Aunt Flo worked downtown although Willow really didn't know what kind of work she did, but it was office work of some kind. Uncle

Gage worked in an office as well but his job was for the railroad as a clerk or dispatcher or such. Both were lucky to have remained employed during the depression and into the war years.

As Uncle Gage stooped down to put the gifts under the tree, Willow's mind whirled to explore the possibilities of one with her name attached. But her thoughts were interrupted by the arrival of Grandma and Grandpa Cain. More packages and jars of Grandma Cain's pickled beets and watermelon slices and her famous fruit cake as well as cream for whipping. Willow's stomach danced joyously at the prospect of all the tasty treats that would adorn their Christmas table.

Indeed, the table was beautiful and groaned under the scrumptious dinner, enhanced only with lots of good conversation and laughter. After the leisurely meal, Grandpa George and Uncle Gage took up residence in the living room while the ladies cleared the table, distributed leftovers and washed and dried the dishes. Willow went about her work quietly, listening to the adult conversation. What was it Grandma Bessie said? *Children should be seen and not heard.* It was a sign of respect. And it was also a way in which Willow learned a great deal. When the women thought no one was listening, Aunt Flo asked Eve if there was news about Zach. Mother just shook her head and both women looked really sad.

Willow went to the living room and sat quietly while Grandpa and Uncle Gage talked.

"This latest campaign doesn't look good, George," Uncle Gage was saying. "I've heard the casualties have been heavy on our side."

"I'll be glad when our boys can come home and the whole mess will be over with. *My* war was supposed to be the war to end all wars."

Willow knew that Grandpa George had served in the army in WWI. There were pictures in Grandma's living room of Grandpa in his uniform and he often told stories about his days overseas.

Uncle Gage continued.

"Forces in Belgium are struggling from all the reports I've heard."

"Our boys have spunk," Grandpa responded. "My money is on the USA troops."

He stopped and the positive attitude of the previous statement seemed to fade as he continued.

"But war is hell no matter how you look at it. We see the big picture, but those fighting men are individuals fighting all kinds of battles within themselves. I know that first hand."

Grandpa George's countenance took on a certain grimness that Willow had never witnessed before.

"I pray Zach can make it through..." Grandpa's voice choked and tears came to his eyes.

His thoughts were sort of suspended as if there was more to say, but the words wouldn't come.

Uncle Gage seemed content in bringing the conversation to a close as both men noticed Willow's interest in the subject matter.

It was almost impossible for Willow to wait any longer for the gift opening. It seemed like everyone was stalling and waiting for who knows what? Grandpa George must have sensed Willow's growing impatience.

"You women ever gonna get those dishes finished?" he raised his voice in the direction of the kitchen. Then he winked at Willow.

Grandma Blanche responded.

"Just hold on," she chided. "Probably nothing there for you anyway since you've not been too good this past year."

Grandma and Grandpa always had this gruffness going on, but Willow knew deeper feelings existed between them. There was the time Grandpa hurt his hand and Grandma carefully bandaged and doctored it. And when Grandma got down with the lumbago in her back, Grandpa did the cooking and carried a food tray to her in their bedroom. When Grandpa worked outside in the summer sun, Grandma was always there to offer him a cool glass of water or lemonade. And Grandpa never missed an opportunity to open doors for Grandma and help her up the steps or into the car. Yes, when all was said and done, Grandma and Grandpa Cain were good for each other.

It was a wonderful Christmas. Willow was delighted with the scarf and hat Aunt Flo had knitted for her. Colors of pink and burgundy went just perfectly with the new gray coat. Everyone applauded as Willow modeled them for the guests. And a pair of new shoes from Grandma and Grandpa Cain! No more feeling the wet, the mud or the cold in her shoes with the holes in them. But even better was the book Grandpa George presented to her. It was a book about horses and Willow was ecstatic.

Grandma Blanche and Aunt Flo seemed really pleased with the hot pads Willow had sewed for them. Mother got a new floral printed apron trimmed with rick-rack from Grandma and a small box of talcum powder from Aunt Flo. Both Uncle Gage and Grandpa George received boxes of homemade chocolate fudge and new neck ties. And mother must have liked the wooden box because she got tears in her eyes when she opened it and Willow caught her later rubbing her fingers over the display of dainty painted flowers. That made Willow happy.

After everyone was stuffed with food and all the gifts were opened and much visiting had taken place, the guests began to leave for their own homes. Grandma and Grandpa left with a plate of leftovers and gifts in their arms and Uncle Gage and Aunt Flo left shortly after that with slices of pumpkin pie and cookies as well as gifts. The house was quiet. Mother left the tree lights on a little longer than usual and Willow sat with her book of horses and her tablet on which she sketched horses running wild and free. Inside, Willow shared the feeling of freedom her drawings represented. It would be a Christmas Willow would remember in years to come.

Chapter Four

Winter days of 1945 seemed to drag on incessantly. Temperatures dipping down several degrees below normal kept Willow pretty much inside once chores were done and the trek to and from school was completed. The new winter coat with the addition of the new scarf and hat helped make the weather a bit more palatable, but Midwestern cold was nothing to take lightly.

Evenings were often spent winding cloth pieces which had been cut into strips and sewn together. These would be taken to a lady they knew who would make them into rag rugs. Some of them were crocheted into rugs by Eve's capable hands and an oversized crochet hook. Nothing could be wasted. And Willow enjoyed putting her bare feet on a woven rug when she got out of bed on cold winter mornings. Winter evenings sitting with a bowl of popcorn listening to old radio transmissions full of static was a memorable time.

Eve quite often quilted in the wintertime, setting up the large quilt frames in the middle of the living room, stretching the fabric as tight as was possible for the best quilting. Willow started her first piece of embroidery, learning how to ply the needle with colorful threads to create designs. She was good at making tiny stitches. When she tired of that, she might play under the quilt frames. There were times when Eve read to Willow such exciting tales as *Tom Sawyer* or *The Adventures of Huckleberry Finn.* Or perhaps Willow would get a good horse story from the library and be lost in it for hours. She might even sketch some horses on excess paper. Mother had cut strips of wallpaper for hanging and there was a 4" roll left over that had separated the strips and Willow used those for drawing. She used crayon and pencil and chalk in her drawings.

The war in Europe continued to rage and was dragging on as well as the winter. December was marked by the Battle of the Bulge. Dense snow falling in the forests of the Ardennes Mountains had only aided the German army attack in Belgium. The Ardennes Mountains were some of the most rugged mountains; and that combined with the cold and snow had taken its toll on American forces. News from the front came slowly to anxious relatives and friends waiting for some good signs that the allies were winning which in turn would mean weary loved ones might be coming home soon.

Willow often caught her mother studying two photos in the house. One was of Uncle Zach and the other was a picture of Daddy. She wanted to ask questions but could not bring herself to possibly upset her mother. Children seemed to have a sixth sense about things like that. Besides, Grandma Bessie would say, *The reason a dog has so many friends is because he wags his tail instead of his tongue.* And Grandma Bessie was probably right. Now was not the right time to be asking questions.

Spring couldn't come too soon. All the food they had worked so hard to store away last summer was being rationed and carefully conserved now. An epidemic of measles broke out among the students at the small neighborhood school and attendance was so scarce that Miss Tyler halted teaching multiplication tables until children returned to school and were healthy enough to study. Willow's contact with the measles resulted in missing a week of school. But she was only really sick for two of those days. She slept a lot during that week and was encouraged with visits from Grandma Cain who brought her a fried chicken leg and from Aunt Flo who brought a book of paper dolls; and although she was getting a little old for dolls, she enjoyed cutting out the outfits and fitting them to the paper doll.

August of 1945 came in with August's usual stifling heat and humidity.

"Hurry, Willow. Aunt Flo and Uncle Gage will be here soon."

"Coming, Mother," Willow answered as she came down the stairs still buttoning the white buttons on her blue and white sun dress.

"It's not often we get the chance to drive into the city."

Willow was excited. Usually a trip to town meant business or groceries and quite often it meant a long walk, but this jaunt was just for amusement, maybe even a moving picture show. And a chance to go for a ride in Uncle Gage's Chevrolet.

"Do you think Uncle Gage will stop for ice cream?"

"That would certainly be a nice treat on a hot day like this, but I wouldn't count on it," Eve responded, brushing back her already damp hair.

Eve and Willow had spent the early morning working in the garden, attempting to avoid the blistering sun rays of a hot August day. Then it had been inside work with the carrying up of canning jars from the basement and while Eve continued to prepare the ripe tomatoes and cooked them, Willow put the cooked ones in the colander with its wooden pestle and turned it around and around to press out the tomato juice. By suppertime, there were 21 jars of tomato juice to be put away in the basement ready for winter soups and other uses. Willow liked the look of the jars of canned vegetables lined up on the shelves...green beans, wax beans, pickles, sweet corn, beets, and sauerkraut.

All day Willow had dreamed of this outing seeing the sights of town. And perhaps an ice cream cone. Glimpses of strawberry or chocolate drifted through her mind as the day progressed. Probably strawberry sounded the best. Yes, strawberry it would be. Surely Uncle Gage would see the need for ice cream on such a hot day.

Uncle Gage's Chevrolet pulled into the driveway and he honked the horn to announce their arrival. Eve and Willow piled into the back seat. Uncle Gage always took good care of his car, his pride and joy, as Aunt Flo called it. Willow was always careful to shake the dirt off her shoes before she got inside the car.

Conversation on the ride into town revolved mostly around the weather and about their aging parents and the garden and about the upcoming school year. Something strange penetrated the air as they approached the city. People alongside the roads seemed to all be converging on the city streets. By the time Uncle Gage found a parking place, people were pouring onto the sidewalks and the level of excitement was reaching new heights.

"What's going on, Mother?" Willow asked, sensing the excitement.

"I'm not sure," Eve responded, as they exited the vehicle. "Stay close."

Willow slipped her hand inside Eve's as they pushed their way into the crowd.

"What's going on here?" Uncle Gage inquired of a well-dressed gentleman.

"End of the war," the man shouted over the growing din.

Could it be at long last? After all the rationing, all the fighting, all the men who had died or were wounded? Was it really over? A fever of excitement and disbelief ran through the crowd as the word was passed from person to person. Shouts of joy and relief rippled through the streets. Hugs were being exchanged between people who didn't even know each other. A newsboy selling newspapers shouted out the good news, making his final transaction for the day with Eve just as he sold out. People armed with pots and pans banged on them with kitchen utensils, creating near hysteria. Eve, Willow in tow, pushed her way to the front of the crowd. People stretching to see the street pushed against them until Willow thought they might lose their footing. A vehicle coming down the street carried the city mayor, waiving his hand and his hat at the crowd. Willow couldn't quite understand everything being said, but he was shouting things like "It's over with! The war is finally over!"

Some people were crying; some were shouting. Some were hugging everyone they came in contact with. Others were dancing in the street while still others continued banging away on pots and pans. Willow covered her ears when they came too close. It was a celebration like no other.

Behind the mayor's vehicle was a group of soldiers, a scraggly looking bunch who marched with weary feet. Willow heard someone say something about them being among the first to return. It was a small group of men, a small representation of the men who had fought so valiantly for so long. Some limped and some were bandaged and all wore serious expressions on their faces, staring ahead as they marched. By this time, Aunt Flo had fought her way through the crowd and was right behind Eve and Willow.

As the soldiers approached, Willow stared into their faces...faces that were grim despite the end of the war, perhaps having seen and experienced too much to be emotional about the war's ending. Eyes stared straight ahead, shoulders slumped in spite of the regimen of marching.

Suddenly Eve's grip on Willow's hand tightened. One soldier in particular had caught her attention as he passed before them.

"Flo," she screamed above the noise. "It's Zach! Is it Zach?"

And had that soldier flinched for just a second? Was there a halt in his step?

Even before the words were out of her mouth, she and Flo were pursuing the group of soldiers, shouting Zach's name. But not one of the group turned in their direction. An overzealous crowd was rapidly cutting him from their view. Excited people pushed against them and inhibited their progress. Eve began to push back against them, trying desperately to get to the street and into an area of less congestion. As if they were trying to impede their progress, the swarm of people began to swallow the two women and the little girl. It took minutes to break loose from the crowd, the sisters standing helplessly staring after the group of disappearing soldiers. Absent from the group was the soldier in question.

"Didn't you see him?"

Eve was emotional.

Flo shook with both fear and excitement.

"I thought it was him," she replied. "Oh, Eve, did you see the look in his eyes?"

"But it *was* him, Flo. I know it was. When I saw him, I had this feeling inside. It's got to be him."

"Do you think he heard us calling his name?"

"I don't know. The crowd is so loud. But once I thought he reacted slightly when I yelled.

"That means he's alive. Where did he disappear?"

"And he's back," Eve surmised. "He made it back."

"We really don't know for sure," Flo cautioned. "We have to be positive it was him."

By this time a very much out of breath Uncle Gage had caught up with them.

"What's going on?" he panted. "You both just started darting through the crowd like two bats out of..." He checked himself, realizing Willow was *listening with both ears,* as Grandma Bessie would say.

Flo found the words.

"We think we saw Zach in the group of soldiers."

Uncle Gage's jaw grew slack in amazement.

"Are you sure? After all this time? Is it even possible?"

"We are pretty sure," Eve answered the question.

"How can that be? We've had no word for...how many months has it been?"

"It *could* happen," Flo was quick to respond.

"So where is he now?"

Eve stammered.

"We don't know. He...he disappeared."

It really did sound unreal. Had the girls been mistaken? Had Eve's enthusiasm just transferred itself over to Flo because they both wanted to believe that their brother was alive and right here in town? Shock set in now and Eve's stomach was experiencing the same kind of nausea it had when the news had come about Chuck.

"What do we do now?" Flo started to cry.

Eve's grip on Willow's hand tightened once more.

"Well, right now I just need to get us out of here," Uncle Gage proposed.

And taking Aunt Flo by the hand, he started back through the throngs towards the car, Eve and Willow following at a quick pace.

The ride in the car was a quiet one, each person in the vehicle alone with his own thoughts. Finally, when they were safely in the security of country roads, it seemed safe to speak.

"No need to get Mom and Dad's hopes up," Flo suggested.

"They've been through enough," Eve added. "We won't tell them. Not yet."

Well, at least that much had been decided. Willow pondered what she'd seen and heard. She hadn't actually seen Uncle Zach in the street, but realized which uniformed man her mother was talking about. She tried to visualize the man and compare it with the photo of him on the shelf at home. The match would not come into view. She settled back against the cloth seats of Uncle Gage's Chevrolet. Like the soldier who disappeared in the crowd, she guessed that any hope of a strawberry ice cream cone had just disappeared as well.

The start of Willow's sixth grade in school was pretty much uneventful. A bit of nostalgia swept through her as she and Alice passed by Miss Tyler's fifth grade room with Miss Tyler acknowledging them with her sweet smile. But she thought Mrs. Canaday's sixth grade room was going to be okay. A windowsill ablaze with potted plants indicated Mrs. Canaday must like flowers; and a table to one side of the room laden with art materials caught Willow's eye at once.

And a colorful bulletin board welcoming students to the sixth grade was pleasing. Yes, this was going to be a good year.

Some of the most notable changes were James Smith's broken arm and Bobby Carson's growth spurt. He was much taller than Willow now and his freckles seemed to have multiplied on his face. Then there was Constance Brown with her new clothes. No surprise there. Willow overheard Connie telling all about the shopping trip she and her mother had taken to Chicago. Big deal! Everyone in the room recognized that Connie Brown was trying to impress Mrs. Canaday on the first day so there would be no mistake as to who was important in the community. Mrs. Canaday, obviously warned ahead of time, seemed to be oblivious to Connie's endeavors to impress. Susie Roberts' hair cut was new and Willow thought it looked real nice. No more braids, just a short wedge. But rumor had it that the entire Roberts family had a lice infestation. Nevertheless, it was an attractive haircut. And there was Bucky Wilson sporting a black eye. No surprise there either. Willow was sure it was one of many and the result of a misunderstanding and that Bucky would deny any wrong doing. All of the kids who were in Willow's fifth grade were back for another year of school. Of interest was a new addition to their class. His name was Frank Castle…and Alice was smitten at first sight.

Books were issued as well as a list of supplies each student should bring on his own. Willow's attention went directly to the reader and then to the history book and was quickly intrigued by them. But, alas, at the bottom of the stack was the menacing arithmetic book and Willow's stomach lurched. Bobby Carson must have noticed because he tapped her on the shoulder and smiled a toothy grin and winked. Somehow that was comforting.

Once Eve and Flo passed through the iron gates to the Veteran's Administration grounds, a feeling of excitement and apprehension enveloped them. Both women knew the history. Established after the Civil War for the benefit of those who served, it stood as a monument for soldiers of the ensuing wars. More recently the facility had become the neuropsychiatric center for returning military men and women. Spacious green lawns stretched as far as the eye could see, benches were occupied by men sitting quietly possibly contemplating how they had arrived at this point in their lives. This would be home for those suffering from the effects of war or those who had no other place to go. A large white gazebo with latticed sides that served as a band shell for weekly concerts during nice weather glistened in the morning sun. Immaculately kept lush flower beds, planted and maintained by the veterans, filled every corner of the property. It was part of their treatment. A small lake for boating sparkled deep hues of blue. Indeed the scene represented peace, a respite from the concerns of life, a well-deserved rest for those who served their country.

Buildings, however, were a bit more imposing, being built of cold brick and stone with tall narrow windows and vines of ivy adorning the outside of the buildings, their façades broken only by the heavy oak doors that marked their entrances. Some buildings were glorified barracks for those who needed medical attention. Bed after bed was occupied by men, some of whom were missing parts of their bodies or were suffering from what was commonly known as being shell-shocked, a term of the day for those unable to cope with the effects of war. Buildings were made to last for all the men and women who would need its service in the terrible war years yet to come. Eve and Flo looked for the administration building.

A dimly lit corridor welcomed Eve and Flo as they stepped onto granite floors. A young woman with upswept hair and a good supply of makeup on her face sat at a nearby desk. She gave them a questioning look as she closed the appointment book in front of her.

"We've come to inquire about a serviceman who has possibly returned recently from the war," Flo clearly stated the reason for their presence.

Giving a hard chew to the gum in her mouth and rolling her eyes as if she had to really think hard about the answer, she finally responded.

"Second door on the left."

Following the red nail polished hand that pointed in that direction, Eve and Flo started towards the second door on the left.

Young men milled around the room. Some sat, some talked quietly and some stood in a line. The sisters chose the line. After what seemed like forever, it was their turn to stand in front of a middle aged woman sitting behind a typewriter. Her short graying hair was unruly, a pencil was lodged behind her right ear at the ready for any immediate use. Piercing and unfriendly brown eyes stared at them over eyeglasses slid half way down her nose. Clearly everyone who stood before her had been sent there to complicate her day. Through a glass window behind her, they could see a gentleman in a suit sitting behind a huge desk poring over papers spread out in front of him. A second woman, a much younger one also wearing glasses, stood at a filing cabinet. She glanced in their direction when the sisters once again stated their problem.

Giving a sigh of impatience, the gray haired woman mumbled something about wasn't everyone looking for someone and that it wasn't her job to find every lost soldier. She merely glanced at the photo of Zach they laid on the desk in front of her.

"We are just too busy with the ones who come every day," she stated. "Your case in not unique and there's not a lot we can do to help."

Anything would have been better than nothing, but this woman had given them all the help she would.

Calling out *Next!* she dismissed the two women in front of her with a wave of her hand.

Picking up Zach's photo, they moved aside in bewilderment as a young man shuffled into the spot they vacated.

"Now what?" Flo asked with tears starting in her eyes.

"Let me think a minute," Eve responded.

"Excuse me."

They turned to see the young woman who had been standing at the filing cabinet.

"This way," she motioned.

When they were comfortably out of view of the gray haired secretary, the young lady removed her glasses to reveal sparkling blue eyes.

"We probably can't help you," she whispered. "There are so many that need help, need processing. We are overloaded with work, but I would like to help."

Eve pushed the photo of Zach into the young lady's hand. She studied the face and then returned it to them.

"He's a handsome young man. Your…?"

"He's our brother," Flo volunteered.

"I can't say that I've seen him," she offered with a sigh. "Like I said, there are so many. But I think I would remember that face. I don't know if it would help or not, but sometimes when these soldiers come back, they can be found at the YMCA, perhaps the Hotel Wolford downtown, local bars."

She hesitated. "Possibly Green Street."

She blushed at that but the sisters understood. They knew what that meant.

"Sometimes local churches offer free meals and some show up there. Also, check with any former girlfriends or buddies he hung out with before he went in."

"Thank you so much…" Eve let her words drift.

She hurriedly scribbled her name and phone number on the back of a scrap of paper and pushed it into the young woman's hand.

"Just in case something comes up," she said.

"My name is Sally," the young girl volunteered, tucking the scrap of paper into a skirt pocket. "I'd better get back. Good luck."

With that, Sally disappeared behind the wainscot wall.

Both Eve and Flo were quiet on the ride back home. Neither had expected this to be an easy thing, but already the walls seemed insurmountable.

"Where do we start?" Eve asked as Flo concentrated on the road ahead.

"Well, Sally gave us several suggestions. More than we had thought of. She was very helpful."

"A lot more than Mrs. Hardnose. Have you ever seen anyone so rude?"

"Yes, but I can see the frustration in her job."

"I'm just saying. No need to be rude."

"What was the name of that girl Zach was seeing last year?" Eve was already thinking.

Flo pulled to stop at a red light. She turned to Eve with a smile on her face.

"Irene, I think," she giggled. "I'd rather start with her than go down on Green Street."

Eve joined in the laughter.

"Let's save that as a last resort."

But Green Street was no laughing matter. It was known for dwelling after dwelling housing ladies often referred to as *ladies of the night.* Most respectable people avoided the neighborhood and might have been surprised at the clientele should they have visited those streets. Men in overalls might make afternoon visits; men in three piece suits preferred the seclusion of the darkness of evening. Red lights clearly marked the houses. If one should appear during the morning hours, they would find very little activity. The streets here rarely came alive until late afternoon. The red light district would indeed be the last resort.

Boys! What good were they anyway? Willow muttered all the way home from school. They always got their way about everything. Boys got to do fun and interesting things. Boys could be anything they wanted. Girls were either nurses or secretaries or teachers. But most of all, boys got in the way of friendships.

Alice was so preoccupied with the new boy…Frank Castle. Who did he think he was? Royalty? Just like his name? Willow knew better than that. After all, hadn't she suffered at the mouth of Connie Brown her entire life over her own name? Well, at least during her school years. Hadn't she been teased about being a tree by that girl time and time again? Well, maybe she was too hard on Frank Castle; but since he came on the scene, there was a clear gap between Willow and Alice.

"Where are you off to in such a hurry?" Mother asked.

"Down by the crick. I think maybe the persimmons might be ripe."

Grabbing a pail, Willow set out in search of the persimmon tree she had checked out earlier. Sure enough the fruit looked to be the ripe deep orange color; and after sampling one of the treasures, she set about filling her pail until her thoughts were interrupted by a sound behind her.

"You startled me," she said, whirling around to see Bobby Carson's freckled face as he laid his bike over on its side.

"Hi, Willow," he said with a toothy grin. "Watcha doin'?"

"Pickin' persimmons," she answered. "Want one?"

"Don't know. Never had them before."

"Here. Try one," she said as she handed him the squishy fruit.

Bobby reluctantly took it and gave her a questioning look.

"People really eat these things?"

"Sure, go ahead. They are great when ripe, but bitter as heck if they're not. Unripe ones can make your mouth pucker."

Bobby cautiously placed the fruit in his mouth.

"Watch out for the seeds," Willow warned. "You can just spit them out."

"Not too bad," Bobby responded, spitting out the seeds and licking his lips. "I've never had one before."

"Well, you should never doubt me. I wouldn't try to fool you on somethin' like that. My Mom makes a really good persimmon pudding. Better now that sugar isn't rationed anymore."

Bobby Carson smiled and walked towards the creek.

"You come here often?" he called over his shoulder.

"Yeah, it's one of my favorite places. Sometimes I look for mushrooms in the spring or maybe watercress out of the crick or sometimes gather wild flowers. In the fall, there's a patch of hazel nuts just over that way. And then sometimes I just sit here and watch the water spill over the rocks and think. And sometimes I pick persimmons."

Bobby seemed amazed.

"Me, too," he replied. "Well, the part about coming here to think. Not picking persimmons," he smiled.

He picked up a grass stem; and running his fingers down its length, stuck it in the corner of his mouth. Willow joined him by the creek. Sun glistening in his eyes seemed to change the color of them. She'd never noticed that before.

"I came here a lot after my Mom died," he mused. "Just a quiet place where I can be alone and try to figure things out."

Willow understood that. She, too, had come here after her Dad's death. It was a place of peace.

"You want me to go so you can be alone?"

"No, no," he exclaimed. "I don't need to be alone now. I kinda like your company."

"Your Mom's been gone a long time now," she began.

He thought awhile and Willow was about to think she had crossed an invisible line when he answered.

"Yeah, four years now."

He paused.

"Sometimes I have trouble remembering her face," he blurted out.

She thought he was maybe going to cry.

"I know that feeling," Willow sighed. "I feel the same about my Dad. Oh, I'll never forget him, but it's just hard to see his face sometimes. I can remember sitting on his lap and him giving me root beer hard candy. And then sometimes I think I can hear his voice. It was always full of laughter."

"I know what you mean. When I remember my mom, I think of how she always read stories to us. I guess I'm lucky. I was old enough to have memories. Not sure Beth and Brian were old enough to remember much."

"You do a good job of taking care of them."

"Thanks. Sometimes it's hard. But I think that's what she'd want me to do."

"It's none of my business," Willow was gentle, "so you can tell me it's not if you want, but how did your mom die?"

"Cancer. At least that's what my Dad said and that was only once. We don't talk about it anymore. And I don't ask 'cause I think it makes him sad."

"Yeah, that's why I don't ask a lot of questions from my mom. She cries about it. Even though she thinks I don't see her."

Bobby shook his head in agreement.

They studied the creek as it swirled and ran free and created little eddies, watched as it tunneled its way around a fallen log or splashed over rocks.

"It makes a pool down the way," he offered. "Wanna see?"

She knew exactly where he meant but she set her pail of persimmons down and skipped after him until they came to the spot where the water seemed to have reached its destination, forming a fair sized basin of clear liquid. They squatted together peering into the depths.

"Look," he pointed. "See…minnows."

Sure enough. Her eyes followed the direction he was pointing and they watched as the miniature fish darted and turned and occasionally surfaced only to disappear once more under little whirlpools.

She nudged him quietly and whispered, "There's a frog."

"Where?"

"There. On that dark rock."

"Oh, yeah, I see it. Isn't it amazing how he blends in so well with everything around him?"

They watched quietly for some time until the frog, apparently tired of sunning himself, hopped down into the water. And then Bobby finally got up and offered his hand to help her stand. She accepted it graciously and felt special that he should extend such a courtesy.

"I need to be gettin' back," he announced. "Dad will be expecting supper when he gets home from work."

He was ahead of her and she noticed the muscles in the calves of his legs as he walked. When they reached the spot where he'd left his bicycle, he said a quick good-bye; and throwing one leg over his bike, sped towards home. Willow picked up the pail of persimmons and started back to the house all the while dreaming of persimmon pudding.

The wooden siding needed painting. But then most everybody's house needed paint in their neighborhood. Willow noticed Bobby's bike on its side near the steps. Her knock on the door brought the face of a small girl to the front window, peeking from behind a white curtain. Then she heard the voice associated with the face from inside the house.

"Somebody's here. I think it's a girl from your school."

"Get back from the door," she heard Bobby say from inside. "And pick up your toys."

Willow smiled at that.

The door opened and Bobby Carson appeared in an apron with flour dusting his face. Willow concealed the giggle she felt inside.

"Hi, Willow."

"Hello, Bobby," she began. "Remember the persimmons?"

"Yeah," he said, suddenly remembering the apron and frantically trying to untie it.

"Well, I brought you some persimmon pudding," she said, thrusting the foil covered package at him.

"Okay, thanks," he stammered. "Uh, I was just fixing supper."

"I see," she smiled.

It wasn't a big house or fancy, but it was clean. A little boy was putting plates and silverware on the table and an adorable little girl was picking up toys and putting them in a cardboard box as she shyly smiled at Willow.

"I gotta keep going on these dumplings."

"Can I help?"

He seemed stunned that anyone would want to help.

"Sure."

After a time, Bobby quietly accepted her presence in the kitchen and Willow worked diligently to help make the supper. Bobby surely needed a break, trying to fill the void left by the premature death of their mother. It didn't seem like work when Willow was there. It seemed like no time at all before mashed potatoes, dumplings, green beans were ready and persimmon pudding was waiting to be served for dessert. After playing a bit with Beth Carson, Willow started the walk back home, feeling lighthearted and content.

Chapter Five

Afternoon shadows were already lengthening by the time Eve Evans stepped onto the small porch at 1545 Spruce Street and knocked on the screen door which rattled at the intrusion. Eve waited a few minutes before she repeated the process, wishing all the time that Zach had not forced her into making this visit. If indeed he had returned from Europe, why hadn't he come home…back to his family?

The smell of cigarette smoke and cheap perfume mixed in Eve's nostrils as Irene gingerly approached the open door.

"Yeah?" she asked as she smoothed back the dyed red hair from her face and took another drag from the cigarette.

"Hello. I'm Eve Evans."

"So?"

This was not going to be easy.

"I believe you know Zach Cain?"

It was part question, part statement.

"I'm his sister, Eve."

Again, the woman before her looked annoyed with the interruption, put her hand on her hip, blew smoke from her lips and waited for more information. The unopened screen door served as a sign that the barrier was not going to be removed.

Eve pushed forward.

"I'm looking for him. I understand that you…"she faltered. "Well, I thought you were…well, perhaps seeing him before he went to the service."

"Yeah, I dated Zachee."

Eve cringed at her brother being referred to by that term. With no more information forthcoming, she decided to press on.

"I was wondering if you have seen him recently? Like since the war has ended? I have reason to believe he is back in the area and I need to talk to him."

A man appeared and stood next to Irene. A dirty undershirt had pulled itself out from the pants he wore and suspenders were draped over his hips. He, too, was smoking and put his arms around the voluptuous Irene and blew smoke into her dyed red hair.

"What's goin' on, sweet lips?" he muttered.

"Just some woman looking for someone I used to know, sweetie. No problem. I can't help her."

Then to Eve, "No. ma'am, I haven't seen your brother. Guess he probably doesn't want to see you either."

With that she turned to the man and putting her arms around his neck, proceeded to kiss him. Eve's stomach lurched. Apparently this interview was over and not at all successful.

None of Zach's friends had seen him either. Devoted sisters checked with Barney down at the gas station, with Aaron who often had been his hunting buddy, with Louie who had been in Zach's senior class and now owned a local grocery store. Lots of people would pass through that establishment. Hank Robertson had yet to return from the service and Jerry Wells would never return. His body stayed on foreign soil. Stace Grant was out of town and Eve was just as thankful that she didn't have to talk to him. A young clerk behind the desk at the YMCA seemed like a very good possibility. He explained how the clientele there were mostly servicemen who had nowhere else to go, but were neat and clean and well, mentally and physically alright. The story was always the same...no one had seen Zach or anyone resembling him.

"Oh, I don't know if I can do this," Flo whined. "What if someone should see us?"

"It's okay," Eve consoled. "Anyone who knows us and sees us here would know differently. Remember, we're here for Zach...and Mom and Dad...and us, too, Flo. If our little brother is back in town, we need to find him. And help him, if we can."

With that, she pushed open the door of the first of the ten bars Flo and Eve visited that afternoon. Met with jeers, indifference and drunks, they still had come up empty at the end of the day. Only one bartender even remotely thought he might possibly have seen the soldier in the photo. And he was not even sure enough to be positive. Of course, all of them promised if they saw a young man fitting the description, they would call the young ladies. But by the end of the evening, Flo and Eve felt as if they had made no headway whatsoever. Even as they exited the last saloon, the feeling was one of despair and little hope that any information would be forthcoming from their efforts.

If indeed Zach Cain had returned from Europe, he apparently did not want to be found.

Nothing was any better than sitting in the middle of your best friend's bedroom, sharing a piece of Juicy Fruit gum with that friend. Things had kind of been patched up between the two girls. Alice spent more time with Willow and Willow guessed Frank Castle wasn't that bad…for a boy.

"Tell me more, Willow," Alice pressed.

"All I know is that she told me she was going to be looking for a job and that I would have to take on more responsibility," Willow explained. "Money is tight and with Dad not being there anymore, I guess she feels like it's something she needs to do."

It was a difficult concept in many ways for two young girls to understand, the impact of the war. Although the war was over, daily chores for them had not changed; the walk to school had not changed. Baths and the washing of hair in rainwater collected in the cistern because that was soft water and made their hair feel soft was still a Saturday evening ritual and Sundays were still devoted to church and family dinners. But Willow realized there was less stress in the community as a whole and she'd heard President Truman's speeches on the radio about the changes the country had been through. Changes were inevitable in everyone's life, she guessed and now there would be more change.

"It's kinda cool," Alice gave it some thought. "After all, we *are* growing up so I guess that means taking more responsibility. And your Mom must trust you a lot."

"I don't mind the cooking. I know how to cook," Willow said proudly. "I can clean. Not sure about the laundry and ironing. But I sure will miss her being there when I get home after school. Oh, yeah, I'm supposed to look after Grandma and Grandpa, too."

Actually, it was more like Grandma and Grandpa could look after Willow, but this sounded better.

"You can do it. It's kinda exciting."

Willow was quiet for a few minutes while she creased her skirt between her fingers.

"You…well...is...? What about Frank Castle?"

Alice was always excited to talk about Frank.

"He is so sweet, Willow. He says the nicest things and he makes me laugh. I really, really like him."

Willow's shoulders sagged with the news.

Alice reached for Willow's hands, taking both of them in hers.

"But he doesn't replace you, Willow Evans," she scolded. "You are and always will be my dearest and best friend."

It was all Willow needed to hear. Alice was right. They were growing up and responsibility came along with that. And with her best friend back to being her best friend, Willow knew everything would be alright.

The First Presbyterian Church was one of the several churches serving free lunches to returning veterans. So far it had been a successful project with more than one hundred men passing through its doors each day. Flo and Eve chose to offer their services to help on Wednesday. Spending the morning with gracious ladies, preparing food was good; but serving those men who came through the line was amazing. Men with unshaven faces and dirty clothing. Distasteful smells if one got too close. But the most chilling experience of all was looking into eyes, vacant as if they were unaware of their surroundings. Eyes that reflected the pain and torture they had seen and experienced. Trying to read the story through their eyes meant recognizing the agony, sometimes fear, sometimes just lost in a world of their own. Most were quiet. Once in a while there would be an outburst of temper. Some reacted nervously if there was a sudden movement or loud noise.

Then there were those who were neat and clean on the outside, but carried secrets they could not share on the inside.

Sometimes one of them would start telling a story either of war time or of something that happened to his unit. Most of the anecdotes were humorous. The more serious ones were usually repressed in their thoughts. Some relived the war, some repressed it, but it left scars both mentally and physically on each and every man. For some, it was terrifying to remember those who had been left behind on foreign soil.

Also disturbing were those men who had remained on the home front, serving as well by picking up jobs vacated by servicemen and by doing without to support the war effort.

Quickly putting the bag of groceries on the cabinet and throwing her coat at a chair, Eve hurried to answer the phone that was ringing as she came in the back door.

"Hello."

A hushed voice on the other end of the line whispered, "Mrs. Evans, this is Sally from the VA. I believe your brother might be standing here in the hallway right now."

"Thank you. I'll be right there."

The words burned in Eve's brain. As her pulse quickened and her mind ran with the possibilities, certain numbness overcame her as well. She continued to function even though she felt she was in an out-of-body experience.

Eve gave no thought of calling Flo at work. There wasn't time. If indeed Zach was there, she needed to get to him quickly. A hundred questions could have been asked of Sally, but Eve somehow comprehended the essence of time. Praying she would not be too late, she wheeled into the parking lot and rushed towards the door. Well, she didn't need to scare him. He could bolt, not expecting to see her.

She stopped in front of the massive oak doors once again and took a deep breath before she calmly opened them. It took a few minutes for her eyes to adjust to the darkness of the hallway. Ignoring the receptionist with the red nails, she continued on her way. Looking around, she spotted the grumpy secretary and quickly scanned the line of men standing there. No familiar faces there. Those sitting? Again, nothing. Perhaps she was too late. Then, peeking around the corner, she locked in on Sally's eyes which beckoned to her to follow. Eve quickly followed Sally, avoiding making any contact with the unsuspecting secretary. Thank goodness, that woman was busy. When they were safely out of hearing range, Sally began to whisper.

"He's in the third room on the right. I asked him to sit in there 'til someone was available to see him, hoping to give you enough time to get here. I do believe this is your brother."

"Thank you," Eve responded, putting her hand in Sally's.

"Please," Sally pleaded. "Understand I could lose my job over this. Please…"

"I understand."

She paused again.

"Also, this man, even though he might be your brother, is a very different man from what you remember."

Looking furtively around, Sally headed back to her desk and a very nervous, hopeful Eve placed her hand on the brass door knob of the third room on the right.

It wasn't at all what Eve had imagined in her wildest dreams. If she was nervous when her hand pressed against the door knob, she was taken aback by what she saw when she entered the room. Sally had been right in trying to warn her, but it in no way prepared her for what she saw. A man she did not recognize stood with his back to her, looking out one of the tall windows. He seemed to be oblivious to the sound of the door opening. A bomber jacket hung loosely on his gaunt frame. Hair protruding from under a GI cap was greasy and stringy resulting from neglect. Zach? Could it be? Was this the little brother she remembered?

Perhaps it wasn't Zach at all. Maybe Sally was mistaken. Easy enough to make an error with so many young men returning from Europe and she only having seen a photograph. No, Zach didn't have any graying hair as this man did. As she turned to once again grasp the brass door knob in preparation for leaving, the man whirled from the window, poised ready for attack. However, he froze in bewilderment as their eyes met for the first time. It was a brief moment of recognition, denial and pain. He neither seemed surprised to see her nor gave the slightest inclination of pleasure in doing so. Eve tensed, unsure of what the next action would be...should be. For a brief moment, she considered the possibility of having to protect herself. It seemed like an eternity passed before she was able to speak.

"Zach?" she hardly recognized her own voice.

It lacked strength and sureness.

At first she thought he would not respond. Continuing to stare at her, he slightly staggered; and grabbing for the chair closest to him, steadied himself with its help. However, his gaze never broke from her eyes. She fully expected him to ask who she was. She grew bolder.

"Zach Evans. Zach, is it really you?"

He appeared to be searching his own mind to validate if he really was the person she was asking about. Putting a shaking hand to his several day's growth of beard, his eyes responded for the first time with recognition.

"Eve?"

The voice she heard was raspy with fear and disbelief. Trembling very similar to that when she was told about Chuck's death and feeling tears sting in her eyes, she took a cautious step forward. In what seemed like a time warp, he, too, shuffled forward. It was then she noticed the leg, his right one, as it dragged behind him.

"Are you hurt?" came the natural response.

She was sorry the moment the words came out of her mouth. He turned his body sideways and for a brief instant she thought he would retreat. In an effort to repair any damage she might have caused, she was quick to respond.

"I am Eve," she paused, searching for the appropriate words. Finally she spoke again.

"And you are my little brother Zach."

His eyes filled with tears as she started towards him. She held out her arms and it appeared he would accept them. She embraced him, not refusing to notice the rankness he exuded, the tremor of his body at her touch, the bony frame of a once healthy young man. As he felt the comfort of his older sister, his emotions overcame him and he began to shake. Eve knew he was sobbing, his head on her shoulder, no longer the little brother who had protected his sister many times over, but the little brother who now needed her comfort and compassion.

Eve pondered her next question carefully, but decided it was something that must be done.

"Will you come home with me?" she asked.

He pulled from her and she saw for the first time how tired he looked as if he hadn't slept in weeks. Lines cut deep across his face suggesting he was much older than he was. And there was a scar over his right eye. Despite his filthiness, she reached a caring hand up to caress his face. After a slight flinch at such tenderness, he relaxed and seemed to enjoy the love she offered him.

"Will you?" she asked again.

He didn't answer her, but nodded his head slightly.

She held out her arm and they walked through the door, Zach leaning heavily upon her, dragging the right leg, apparently in pain.

Eve searched for Sally when they passed the front desk, but did not see her. She needed to thank her for her thoughtfulness, but the most immediate concern right now was to get Zach home.

Uncle Zach ruined Christmas that year. It started after the Christmas dinner was over and most of the gifts had been opened. Talk of the war and its effects on him got out of hand. Grandpa Cain was probably mostly at fault for not keeping his own war stories under control. War memories for him did not harbor the same stress they did for Zach. It was apparent that no one understood what Zach had been through. His war experiences had left him desolate, unable to cope with the devastation his eyes had witnessed; and although there were times he seemed like his old self, there were other times the darkness overtook him and he became despondent or cried or was angry. This Christmas it escalated beyond control.

Perhaps it was the time of year…the December Christmas day, this one that reminded him of the one he'd spent in the cold of Russia during the Battle of the Bulge when he lost several buddies within several minutes and he thought he would die as well and later wished he would have. Finally help came in the form of allied troops and he was pulled out and taken back to England. But he left part of himself there amid the bloody bodies and still heard the cries for help from fellow soldiers in his nightmares and their pleas for help from the pain and torture they felt.

There were times when he struggled to separate his war life from his civilian life. Sometimes at night he woke up in a cold sweat, screaming for help for himself and for others. He felt guilt for having made it back to civilization…whatever that might be. He felt anger. Shooting his share of the enemy had become a necessity he deplored. Not because of the principles of the war. He agreed with those. But the knowledge that most of those men were just like him, lonely and cold and wishing as much as he that they were back home with family and friends, was always with him.

To make matters worse, he realized that other people thought he was crazy and often questioned that himself.

No one remembered the exact trigger, but there it was. If anyone had been paying attention, they would have seen it in Zach's eyes or observed the nervousness and irritability that overcame him, but they didn't. The first indication was his outburst.

"None of you know what you're talking about…not any of you!" he yelled, leaning forward in his chair.

He certainly had their attention. A quiet room of people focused on Zach.

"It was hell, don't you know? Pure hell. Grenades going off in front of us, shells landing right beside us…sometimes on us. Dead bodies all around and those that weren't dead were laying there screaming for help. Do you know what it's like when someone is crying out for you to help them and there's not a damn thing you can do about it? Have you ever looked in the face of someone pleading with you to just shoot them and put them out of their agony? And all the time, you're expected to pull yourself together and keep shooting at the enemy! So many injured we had blood all over us and you never knew if it was your own blood or the blood of the fella next to you."

He paused to look at the horror stricken faces before him, but he wasn't seeing them. He was seeing the faces of his comrades in battle.

"We were just kids…not prepared for this kind of thing. There was Buzz who was first in our platoon in almost every kind of athletic thing they put us through and there he was laying at my feet with his eyes wide open and not breathing. And there was Davidson who was the kindest guy ever, always encouraging us to do our best and he's propped up against his gun with half his body shot off. And Kincaid who cried like a baby the first week of boot camp but now he found the courage to run from one soldier to another trying to offer assistance. And the noise…deafening, but no matter how loud the bursting shells were, you could still hear the screams of the dying. Bright flashes of light when the bombs exploded that lit up their faces to show you how alone you probably were. Everybody yelling orders. And we just continued pulling those triggers…over….over and over again. Sarge yelling at us to keep firing and then his voice was silent and someone else started yelling the orders and you knew…you knew…that Sarge was gone, too.

And no matter how much we kept pumping ammunition in them, it seemed like they never stopped coming. And then it got silent for some reason and when the smoke cleared, it was time to take count."

Here Zach paused and tears came to his eyes and slid down his cheeks and his voice was soft and low.

"Copters coming in. Copters coming in!" he shouted. "And whose were they? Theirs or ours? Waiting to see the symbol on the side. Then an American shout and we knew we were going to be rescued. It wasn't a difficult retrieval. Most of what was left was dead bodies. We stacked as many as we could aboard and then climbed in ourselves. It was a quiet ride back behind the lines. Nobody had anything to say and somehow that was worse than the constant noise of the enemy guns.

There were only three of us that made it out. Three out of the entire damn platoon! Three! And why did *we* make it when the others didn't? Live with that, why don't you?"

With that, he stomped from the house and was gone again for a while. Willow had seen her mother cry and once she saw Grandma Cain cry, but she had never seen Grandpa Cain with tears. Still shocked from the outburst, Willow didn't know who to try to console first. Eve and Flo went to their mother, so Willow sat next to Grandpa Cain and put her arm around him.

Grandma Cain cried when she saw her son go through the suffering. Grandpa Cain couldn't figure out how to reach out to his son. Flo tried to reason with her brother. Uncle Gage couldn't really understand. He'd never gone to any war. Eve offered support to him, but when these outbursts occurred, Zach would leave and be gone for anywhere from three days to a couple of weeks. No one knew if he would ever come back. Usually when he did return, he was dirty and unshaven and reeked of cigarette smoke and booze. One thing he never did. He never came back drunk. Never talked about where he'd been. No explanation, but at least he kept coming back.

He obviously had sought help from some place because one day in late spring, he brought a girl home with him who Eve recognized as Sally from the Veteran's Administration Offices. Willow liked Sally and thought she was good for Uncle Zach. He was talking about going to college under the GI bill which provided financial assistance for those who had served in the military. Probably that was partly Sally's influence. He even asked Sally to marry him. Then he disappeared again and was gone for three weeks according to conversations Willow overheard between Eve and Sally and Aunt Flo.

News spreads quickly when there are problems and it wasn't long before students at Willow's school knew her uncle had returned from the war and he was one of the ones who went crazy. Shell shock they called it or maybe battle fatigue or combat exhaustion. Whatever its label, it affected everyone he came in contact with. The war was officially over. The gun fire was silenced. But it thrived in the lives of those who endured it. Stories grew by leaps and bounds and Willow found herself trying to defend her uncle's behavior.

"I knew you'd be here."

Refreshing green color peeking from the buds on the white ash along the banks of the creek seemingly had waited for this moment to burst forth with the promise of spring. Willow turned, not at all surprised by the sound of Bobby's voice. It somehow felt appropriate, not because she expected it but because this was his place of consolation as well. Approaching her side cautiously, he, too, stood for a time, taking in the scene…the winding creek overflowing with spring rains bubbling past rocks as if they were not obstacles. Occasionally, a piece of ice floated by as a reminder of what once was.

Bobby noticed a limb bent and broken by the weight of the winter's snows. Bits of undergrowth were starting to emerge and he was sure if he looked hard enough, he could find an early flower struggling to be set free. Perhaps there might still be some toothwart with its white flowers and its ragged edged leaves. Purple violets could be hiding under last fall's collection of leaves. Maybe even some bloodroot which got its name from the red sap that flowed from its stem when picked. Bluebells and trillium would be right on the heels of these flowers. Most people never bothered to pick early flowers anyway. It was just a delight to discover them after the winter's drabness.

A red cardinal called from its perch in the willow tree with it draping branches; and pair of brown thrashers chirped their thanks for the end of the winter. None of it went unnoticed by the two intruders on nature.

"It's spring," she finally responded. "The whole woods is waking up after a winter's nap."

"I like spring," he said, picking up a fallen branch and breaking off its twigs to make a walking stick. "It's like God promised all along that it would come and now he's making good on that promise."

She thought a minute and then looked at him and nodded in agreement. She moved along the bank of the creek and he turned to walk with her.

"Connie Brown is a mean person," he announced.

When Willow was quiet, he continued.

"She don't always know what she's talking about."

"She has no right. My Uncle Zach acts weird alright. Sometimes he gets very, very angry. Sometimes he's sad. My Mom says he's reliving the war. Who knows? Maybe he *is* crazy. And you know where they send crazy people. They lock them up."

Willow's words ended with a choking back of tears.

He chose his words carefully.

"That's what I heard. Don't know for a fact."

They continued to walk in silence.

"He ain't never hurt you, has he?"

"Nope. Sometimes he tells me stories when he's in a good mood. If he's not, well, I just stay away from him. Mom says that's the best thing to do. It's like he sometimes slips back into another world. The one that's the war. Like he's caught somewhere in between two worlds."

"I wouldn't want you to get hurt."

They both were quiet for a few minutes. They stopped to watch a turtle basking in the sun on a rock.

"I don't think people should talk about your Dad either," he offered.

"I've never told anyone this before, but I've always felt like there is something weird about my Dad's death. But I don't want to upset my Mom by asking questions."

"Yeah."

Again there was silence.

"See that rock?" Bobby asked. "And see how the water splits and goes around it and comes back together on the other side? That's you and me, Willow. No matter what rocks life throws at us, we are like that crick. Our paths are diverted for a while, but we come back just as strong on the other side of the obstacle."

She wanted to tell him that he had a way of making her feel better, but couldn't get the words formed so she just smiled and nodded.

"Come on," he said, "I know where there's a sassafras tree and we can get us some roots for some tea. My Dad says that'll clean up your body real good after the winter."

He found the tree and pulled at a sapling until he had exposed the roots, and digging around them with his pocket knife, broke them off and each one took sassafras root home for making tea. As Willow sipped hers and thought about their conversation, she decided maybe *some* boys weren't too bad. And, as for Connie Brown, well, there was always another day.

Autumn was quickly approaching. Eve sat on the porch swing, absorbing some of the last rays of sun, mulling over the past few years. Everything with the job was working out. She liked the work and really enjoyed pay days and the things money had afforded them; and Willow was doing a good job helping around the house. Dad was having issues with his heart and Mom was becoming fragile.

Just now it was pleasant to sit and enjoy this time of year she enjoyed so much, just something special about the color, the atmosphere, the smells, the memories. Making note of the brilliant splashes of color becoming visible in the trees, she closed her eyes and pictured another autumn season.

"Hey, you awake, Babe?" Chuck asked as he teasingly tugged at the blankets covering Eve.

"Umm," she moaned, turning on her side away from him.

"I'm still asleep."

He turned towards her and took her in his arms, inhaling the fragrance of the shampoo she used in her hair.

"Okay," he said, patting her hip. "I'll just go ahead and call Jerry and see if he wants to go hunting today. It's a glorious fall day out there."

He turned, pretending to get out of bed, but she turned also and pulled him back to her.

"Now that's not gonna happen," she cooed as she tugged at his T-shirt.

She kissed him tenderly and he settled beside her, wondering how he had gotten so lucky.

"Charles Evans, man of my dreams, you have fulfilled every dream I ever had. I can't put into words what you mean to me. Just when I think I've reached the farthest depth of love I can, you take me to a new level."

"That's because I love you. Because we love each other. God knew we'd be the perfect match. And we are, you know. That precious little girl in the next room is proof of our love."

He continued to kiss her, continued to whisper words of love in her ear until a tiny cry in the next room pierced the air.

Eve giggled as she caressed Chuck's face.

"Your perfect little love is calling," she laughed.

She sighed as she got out of bed, wrapping her robe around her.

"Hey," he said, stretching out in the bed. "I was just kidding about going hunting."

"Yeah, yeah," she called back.

"Honey, does this mean I don't get any breakfast this morning?" he called after her.

He fell back against the pillows for a few more minutes, his head resting on his arms extended above him, thinking once more about his girl, his precious Eve, the one who inspired him and made him feel on top of the world.

Chapter Six

Television was the new rage. Moving pictures right there in your own house. No more having to get dressed up or travel to the movies. Just turn it on, adjust the antenna attached to the top of the house, tune the channels and you could watch the Arthur Godfrey hour in the daytime, the Ed Sullivan variety show on Sunday nights, the Jackie Gleason show on Saturday evening. Game shows and nightly news and old movies. Stations signed off every night with the national anthem and the screen went to a test pattern until the following morning. It truly was an age of miracles. Aunt Flo and Uncle Gage were the first to get a television set and Eve and Willow spent many Saturday evenings there where they watched black and white movies while munching on freshly popped corn. It wasn't long before a new set was delivered to the Evans' household.

Eve's job had permitted the luxury of such things plus a newer vehicle had been purchased and Willow had additions to her wardrobe just in time for her entrance to high school. What fun it had been to shop for a new dress, two new skirts, three blouses and a cardigan sweater plus a pair of black and white saddle shoes. Aunt Flo had said those were a *must.* And while Alice and Willow were on a shopping spree of their own, Willow selected some neck scarves and some pop it beads. No need to buy hair clips. Willow's hair was still a mass of curls while Alice's went from braids to pony tail.

"Oh, come on, Willow," Alice challenged. "It will be fun."

"I don't know," Willow was reluctant. "I don't even know how to dance."

Alice slurped a spoonful of ice cream as they sat on the high stools at the dime store food counter sharing a banana split.

"It will be after the football game and I swear we can leave early and have you home by 10:30."

"But you'll be with Frank and where will that leave me?"

"We won't be together all the time. He hangs out with the guys some and he's not real keen on dancing."

Willow wiped the trace of ice cream from her mouth as she digested the last of the pecans and syrup from the bottom of the banana split dish.

"That makes two of us," she sighed. "But, okay, I'll try it."

"Good," Alice seemed satisfied and swiveled the stool back towards the counter.

But Willow wasn't through yet.

"I can't stay any longer. I have a test to study for."

Alice gave a little gasp.

"Gosh, Willow, you study all the time. Relax and have some fun once in a while."

"Mom has her heart set on sending me to college so I can't let her down. I need to keep up my grades."

"You *do* make good grades," Alice replied.

Willow shook her head in resignation. All Alice wanted to do was to marry Frank as soon as they graduated high school and have a whole houseful of kids.

Alice gave another twirl of the food counter stool and hopped down to the floor.

"Come on," she said. "We need to find you some new lipstick. Let's brighten you up a bit."

"Don't know why," Willow said shyly. "I think I look just fine."

"Just fine isn't good enough. You are going to make an impression."

Willow wasn't sure just who she was going to impress or even how to make an impression, but she would humor Alice this once. The *who* came about quite suddenly when Jeff Templeton asked her to dance in the school gym after the football game.

Jeff was a popular student, good looking and a leader in the junior class. If Willow denied the fact she was flattered, she would have been lying. She didn't think she took a breath between the minute he'd asked her to dance until he walked her back to her friends. And if he had given her time to think about it, she probably would have refused; but he was so suave and smooth, she didn't have time to think. She would probably have panicked if she had taken the time to think about the significance of a popular guy asking her, a shy junior who had never ever had a date and had only practiced dance steps with her best friend, Alice in the seclusion of Alice's living room. She might have wondered about it if she could have made her brain slip into action, but all she could do was to maintain her arms around his shoulders. She could have noticed the group of girls who had been passed up, standing in awe of this unpopular girl, this shy girl, this girl who seldom had been seen at after game dances let alone a girl who Jeff Templeton had chosen to be his dance partner.

Alice could hardly wait until Willow returned.

"What was he like?" she whispered.

Willow didn't answer. Instead she was lost in a flood of emotions and could not find any words that would suitably express her feelings. Actually, her thoughts were only of finding a seat and sitting down until the wave of dizziness she was feeling had passed. But instead, she just stood with a smile on her face while Alice, Frank, Bobby and a few other kids from south of town clustered around her.

Alice gave up on the answer to her question as to what it was like to be dancing with Jeff Templeton and quickly changed it to, "Are you okay, Willow? Willow, are you okay? Can you hear me?"

As if in a fog, Willow finally found her voice.

"I'm okay. Yeah…I think I'm okay."

But she wasn't alright. There was a buzz in her ears and she was sure her face was a bright red color and her breath came in short gasps. She tried to act nonchalant, like Jeff Templeton was an everyday happening, like it was just a part of her everyday life to have the most popular guy in the junior class dance with her.

"What did he say to you?" Alice needed to know.

Say? She couldn't remember. Did he say anything? Surely he must have said something; but for the life of her, all she could remember was him holding her close and the smell of his after shave lotion. Did he say something? What would he have said? What would make sense? Actually, nothing was making sense to her right now. But surely he said something.

"Oh, just casual talk," she responded.

"Willow, do you know that right now you are the envy of every girl in this gym?"

It was only then Willow looked around the room. It was true. Little clusters of girls stood around the room looking in her direction and whispering. It was a frightening experience.

"They look like they hate me."

"Oh, they probably do. Every girl in here would simply die to dance with Jeff. Girl, you are the topic of conversation for sure."

Scanning the dance floor for a glimpse of Jeff, she found him dancing with a red headed girl. That settled her a bit. So she was not going to be his main focus this evening. In one sense, she was relieved. In another, she felt a wee bit of disappointment.

"Well, Jeff Templeton needs to see how popular you are. Here, dance with Frank," Alice was saying, pushing her into Frank's arms.

So once again Willow was on the dance floor, feeling out of place. Frank was not the dancer Jeff had been and was just as uncomfortable as she was. Maybe awkward was a better choice of words. Being in the arms of her best friend's boyfriend seemed a bit strange.

"Alice gets carried away sometimes," she offered, hoping to put Frank at ease.

Frank accidently stepped on her toe.

"Sorry," he apologized. "I'm not too good at this."

"Me, neither," Willow added and felt somewhat more comfortable.

"Sorry you got dragged into this," she said. "Alice gets carried away once in a while."

Well, hadn't she just said that? How addled could she be?

Willow and Frank were both relieved when the music stopped and they could walk back to the group of friends who were still standing in the same little cluster.

"You are making all kinds of excitement around here, Willow," Alice whispered. "Everyone is talking about you and Jeff."

Willow sighed and pretended it was no big deal, but inside she still had the little aches of excitement herself.

"I'm headed to the bathroom," she whispered back. "Keep your ears open and catch me up on everything you hear."

It was there in the bathroom stall of the high school that Willow met reality. Three girls came in after she had and were busy chatting. Under the stall door, she could see three sets of shoes. The girl who wore the black flats was the first to speak.

"So what is up with Jeff, Susan? I've never seen him like this. Did you two break up?"

Willow was not able to identify that voice. The one responding must have been Susan Sands whose name had been associated with Jeff's for quite some time. In most students' minds, they were linked as going steady.

"Oh, we have a very open relationship. He can do what he wants and I can do what I want. Why, just last week Joe James and I had hamburgers at the Hamburger Hut. It's okay."

Somehow Susan's explanation didn't sound all that convincing.

The third pair of shoes spoke up, the pair of white bucks, a suede shoe, popular among the more elite students.

"Well, all I know," she said, "is that if I had a hunk like Jeff Templeton in my life, I wouldn't be sharing him with *anyone* else."

Willow knew that voice. She didn't even have to guess who belonged to those white bucks and that voice. It was no other than Connie Brown, still causing trouble no matter where she went. She had long since left her associates from elementary school, working very hard and long to be accepted by the students from the *north side* of town.

"So why did he choose *that* girl to dance with tonight? Is he trying to make you jealous?"

This from the girl in the black flats.

"Maybe."

"Oh, I know her," Connie supplied the information. "I went to elementary school with her. She's nobody. Her name is Willow. Can you imagine? Named after a tree? We used to call her *Weeping Willow* because she cried a lot. And her father, well, he killed himself. Sad, isn't it? Anyway, her uncle is in a mental hospital. Just best to stay away from families like that. They all must be crazy."

There was agreement and some laughter here and Willow was pretty sure it came from all three girls.

Unwilling to let it go, Connie went on.

"I think he chose the most unpopular girl he could just to get to you, Susan. He surely couldn't have any other reason for dancing with her right in front of you."

Susan replied, "I never thought for a moment he'd be interested in her in anyway. He'll come crawling back to me. He always does."

"He'd be a fool to do anything else."

Tears came to Willow's eyes. She waited a comfortable amount of time after she heard the door to the bathroom close and before she had courage enough to open the stall door. While washing her hands at the sink, she looked at herself in the mirror. Why would Jeff have had any other reason to choose her than to embarrass her and possibly upset Susan. Willow needed to get away. She entered the gym, scanned the crowd in search of someone, anyone who could help her.

She started towards the group of boys from south of town. Ignoring Frank and the rest of the guys standing in a tight knit group, she walked straight to Bobby Carson.

"Can you take me home?" she pleaded "…now."

There was something about the urgency in her voice that made him keep his questions to himself. He simply turned and followed her.

She turned back to Frank.

"Tell Alice I'm going home."

They found Bobby's car in the parking lot, parked next to Jeff Templeton's convertible. Bobby's car was a jalopy. He had bought it cheap and worked on it every day after school to hold it together to keep it running. He laid a blanket over the hole in the front seat passenger's side before she got in and then went to the other side to start the engine. They pulled out of the school parking lot and he steered the car towards the south of town.

"You want to talk about it?" he ventured.

"No."

Her reply was quick and blunt.

Okay, she didn't want to talk. That was okay. He'd had times he didn't want to talk either. So he drove on in silence, occasionally stealing a glance at her profile. Something was really bothering her.

Only one other bit of conversation took place during the five mile ride.

"Sorry you had to leave the dance," she said without emotion.

"It's okay," he replied. "I'm not much into dancing anyway."

He only knew of one place to take her so he drove to the creek. She didn't seem to object if she comprehended where they were at all. He pulled the car to a stop and turned off the lights and they sat in silence. A full moon shed its light on the beautiful spot. Its light made the creek appear like a silver ribbon running through the lightly wooded area. Tops of trees were silhouetted against the lighter colored sky. The weeping willow could be seen draping its branches down to the river bank.

He wondered how long she would stay quiet. It seemed like an eternity.

"Do you think I'm stupid?" she finally asked.

It wasn't the question or comment he expected to hear.

"Uh, no," he faltered but grew bolder with each word. "I've known you a long time, Willow, and I've never thought of you in those terms. As a matter of fact, I think you're pretty smart...and talented."

He waited.

"Well, I was stupid tonight."

This was not going to be easy.

"How do you figure that?" he asked cautiously.

"Jeff Templeton," she raised her voice. Then in a softer voice, "Jeff Templeton."

"Yeah," he drawled, waiting for more information.

"He made an idiot out of me," her voice cracked with emotion.

"And how did he do that?"

He waited for an outburst, thinking that was probably not a response she wanted to hear.

"He used me. He used me to make Susan Sands jealous."

Oh, my, he thought. *I am just making things worse. Perhaps making her mad would take her focus off herself.*

"Weren't you watching the whole thing?" she snapped.

"Yeah, I didn't know you could dance."

"Ooh," she stammered. "You're missing the whole point."

The corners of his mouth tuned up as he smiled at her gusto.

"Then enlighten me."

She was quiet again and he was sure he'd said all the wrong things.

"The willow tree is beautiful, isn't it?" he attempted to change the subject.

"Beautiful? How can you say that?" she stormed. "I heard her say it again tonight. It was bad enough to have her tease me my entire life about my name, but when she did it again tonight, well, I could have scratched her eyes out. She said my parents named me after a tree and that she and her friends called me *Weeping Willow* because I was always crying."

At that she began to sob and searched through her purse for a handkerchief which she found and blew her nose loudly. She realized she was making Connie's point for her by crying.

"I think it's time you started at the beginning and told me the whole thing," he suggested.

She sighed. Where to start? But she did. Slowly she told him the whole thing, how she was flattered by Jeff's attention until she overheard the conversation in the girls' bathroom. Bobby studied her as she talked and his mind wandered from time to time as he noticed the cute way she rolled her eyes when she talked or the way they danced when she was excited. The moonlight on her face gave a strange glow that worked magic in his chest. Once or twice he wondered what he could say to his friend that would make her feel better. And then he realized she had quit talking.

"Well?" she was saying.

"I can't say what Jeff or anyone else thinks," he began. "I just know that you are a wonderful person. You have a lot more to offer than Connie or Susan or any of those other girls. If Jeff is cold enough to play those kinds of games with a nice girl like you, he doesn't deserve even one dance with you. And what you do with all of this is your choice."

He sat quietly for some time.

"And what is it that Grandma Bessie always says? *Some people will always throw stones in your path…It depends on what you do with them…"*

Willow finished it.

"…build a wall or build a bridge."

She thought about it. And, knowing Bobby like she did, he had said what he thought and that was all he would say. Then she suddenly realized that her anger was gone. She didn't even feel like crying anymore. But he had one more thing to say.

"Willow, without saying anything, just look at the willow tree," he asked.

She turned to look and almost opened her mouth to speak. He touched her lips with his fingers to keep her from saying anything. And didn't he know that would be difficult for her to do?

"The willow tree is strong. Yet its branches float gracefully in the wind. They bend but they do not break. They weather the most difficult of storms and still survive in all their beauty."

He paused. His hand covered hers.

"You are just like that tree, Willow. You are beautiful, graceful, strong and will bend, but won't break. I love your name and all it represents. Willow, Willow, Willow."

He clearly made his point. She was speechless. They both sat staring straight ahead for several minutes before he sighed and spoke.

"Of course, Mrs. White our fourth grade teacher, probably used willow switches to discipline her students."

She looked at him. He shrugged his shoulders.

"I'm just sayin'."

And then they laughed, the laugh of good friends who care about each other.

Chapter Seven

She would remember this day for years to come. There was something about the chill in the air, something about the way her mother looked, something about the rocks that tumbled in her stomach as she anticipated confronting her mother. Yes, things in her future would trigger memories of this day. Maybe things were best left to rest.

Although that very well could be the solution, burning questions had haunted Willow now for some time. After all, she wasn't a child anymore. A sixteen year old girl was practically a grown woman. In another year or so she would be graduated from high school and going off to college. It was time to ask the questions.

Eve was in the kitchen, apron tied around her tiny waist, her taffy colored hair now beginning to be streaked with some lightness of gray. She wore it in a more fashionably short cut these days which made her look more professional. Glasses were now a permanent fixture on her face; but her eyes still reflected the kindness they always had, the love she felt for her daughter. And her laugh was the same, despite all the issues with Zach's stress over the war and Grandma and Grandpa Cain's health issues. As Eve stood at the sink, Willow drank in the moment. Eve would always be at home in her kitchen and Willow would always picture her there with mingling memories of stories being told and laughter being shared and delicious aromas that always emanated from that room.

"Hi, Mom."

"Oh, hi, Willow. I didn't hear you come in. Supper's not quite ready yet. I was late getting home from work today. How was your day?"

Willow understood she was about to change this happy scene, but she pressed forward.

"Mom," she said quietly, stepping a bit closer to her mother. "I need to ask you something."

"Okay," Eve answered, "but can you talk and set the table at the same time?"

Willow postponed her questions while she took the plates and glasses from the cupboard and began placing them on the table.

"Put plenty of napkins on, too," Eve coached. "Spaghetti always has a way of getting messy."

The words were not going to come easily.

Then Eve paused, wiping her hands on her apron.

"You wanted to ask something?"

"Yes, Mom, I need..."

Eve turned down the boiling water and took a seat at the table.

"Mother, I need to know about my father."

Eve looked a bit stunned.

"What do you want to know? I've always told you he was a fine man and he loved you very much. He loved *us* very much."

"I need to know how he died."

If there was a tiny gasp in her body, Eve struggled to hide it.

"Well, he was killed in an automobile accident. That's public record."

"And?"

Willow wanted to know more.

"That's about all there is to it," Eve avoided looking at her daughter's face.

"Why would Connie Brown say that he took his own life then if that's all there is to it?"

Looking into Willow's eyes, Eve realized that Willow would not relent until she knew the truth. In that way, she was very much like her father. Giving an audible sigh, she began the whole story.

"Your Dad decided he needed to do his part in the war so he enlisted. It was really the only thing we ever had words over. Oh,

I understood his patriotism, but you were small and I wanted him home, not fighting somewhere a long way away from us. He had been to boot camp and was back for a couple of weeks. His friends wanted to take him out for one last night on the town. I remember that he kissed both of us goodbye…you and me…and told me he wouldn't be late. And I believed that because, at that time, I just knew there was a perfect ending to everything in the world. He didn't come home early and although I was concerned, I went on to bed after I'd put you down for the night. Sometime later there was a policeman at the door and he was saying things that just could not be true. Going too fast. Missed the curve in the road."

"But that doesn't explain why Connie said he killed himself."

Eve was crying now and continued through the tears.

"They said…they said…they said there was a suicide note. That he was a coward and couldn't face going into the war. Had changed his mind."

It wasn't what Willow thought she would hear. The words fell on her ears, her ears that were denying what was being said. She heard them, but she couldn't comprehend them.

Was the man she loved and called *Daddy* really a coward? Was he what they said he was?

"I never knew your father to be cowardly about anything. It never made sense to me. How could he have wanted to die when we were so happy? And we wanted other children, too. We had plans for the future…a future together. But there was the note saying he was sorry, he just couldn't face it anymore."

Willow refused to let it go.

"And Grandma and Grandpa Evans? What about them? Why do we never see them and where are they?"

Eve played with the hem of her apron and she formed her words carefully.

"They were humiliated with the idea of suicide as well as trying to grieve. People are cruel and there was a lot a talk and disgrace for them in the community. They blamed me I guess in a way and it was too painful for them to be associated with us. I guess it brought back painful memories for them. They were very bitter. The last I knew they were over in Graceville…about fifty miles east of here. I did try to talk with them, but I guess my own grieving stood in the way."

A cloud descended over Willow as she watched her mother's small body shake with the emotion of remembering. Had Willow done the right thing in bringing all of this pain back to her? Did she really have to know the details? The answer was yes. If Willow was to go on with her life, she had to know the facts and perhaps there she would find the answers.

Willow had been so small when Chuck Evans was killed. Her memories faded more quickly than those of her mother. And Eve had never, ever had a relationship with any man since Chuck's death. For the first time in her life, Willow felt like the strong one who needed to comfort her mother…comfort her for causing the painful memories to surface, comfort her for the loss of Eve's one and only true love.

Sixteen-year-old girls are old enough to get a driver's license and old enough to be employed. After placing applications at Woolworth's 5 and 10 cent store, two women's dress shops and a department store, they were able to obtain jobs. Both would be working at the dime store…Alice behind the lunch counter and Willow at the candy and nut counter. So for the entire summer the two girls walked from their houses to town. Pay wasn't that great, but it was neat to get a paycheck and Willow added to her bank account each pay day.

The supervisor was impressed with the friendly atmosphere Willow created at her station and how quickly she made the correct change and was accurate with the weighing of the candy and nuts. She was never idle and kept her area neat and clean. There were other clerks who didn't do as well and were let go from their jobs.

Alice had her difficulties at the lunch counter. People were not always pleasant when their food was too cold or too hot or on occasion burned. And Alice wasn't that great when it came to making change so she was reprimanded some.

At any rate, both Willow and Alice were successfully employed until the third week of August, just before they started their senior year of high school. Willow was saving for college; Alice was saving to get married.

"Can you help her, Willow?" Bobby wanted to know. "I just don't know anything about stuff like this and she's real emotional about it. I can give you the money Dad set aside for her, but she just doesn't want my help."

"Sure, Bobby, I'd be glad to help out. Ask her if she could go to town with me on Saturday."

Little sister, Beth Carson, was growing up. Brother Bobby, although he had done a good job of taking care of the little family and cooking and cleaning and doing a lot of things Mama would have done if she'd lived, he just wasn't that great at picking out clothes for little girls. And Beth Carson now wanted different things than what he thought was okay.

Willow borrowed the car and picked Beth up on Saturday morning. Bobby gave Willow the envelope with the designated money in it. Beth was quiet at first but the more Willow talked, the more Beth opened up. Willow noticed Beth's beautiful blue eyes and how pretty she was when she smiled. And when she talked, her face lit up and she was simply gorgeous. It wouldn't be long before Bobby would have more issues than just buying clothes for Beth.

It was a grand day. Willow had lots of experience with finding clothing sales and also understood the importance of popular-type clothing so she was able to find some really nice things at bargain basement prices. She enjoyed how Beth began to look for sales as well and also developed her keen sense of matching items of clothing. Willow was pleased when all was purchased at how many outfits they were able to put together. And she could tell Beth was pleased as well.

"Let's stop by the luncheon counter at the dime store," Willow suggested, "and I'll treat you to an ice cream sundae."

"Oh, Willow," Beth smiled. "This has been a wonderful day. Bobby sure knew what to do and who to ask."

"Yeah, your brother is a good guy."

Beth smiled and relished the chocolate sundae before her.

"Thanks, Willow," Bobby said. "Guess I'm not much at being a mother."

Willow smiled.

"Yeah, but you make a pretty good big brother."

Jimmy Graves asked Willow to the junior-senior prom. They had been on a few dates prior to the prom, so it wasn't all that much of a surprise. Of course, Alice and Frank would be going together and they would double date, going to a fancy restaurant first and then to the dance. Prom was held in the school gym which had been transformed for the occasion by a decorating committee under the direction of no other than Connie Brown.

Willow hadn't been to a dance since the one after the football game last year. Jimmy didn't know anything about that incident or about her history with Connie Brown which was just fine. Alice and Willow had gone to a shop in the next town and found the perfect dresses. Willow's dress was lavender tea length with lavender lace over the bodice and Jimmy had gotten her a wrist corsage to match. Alice had chosen a pale green with a full skirt that stood out with crinoline slips. It took both of them to get her in Frank's car. The girls had shopped together and

Willow was to wear the same dress in a couple of weeks or so when she would be maid of honor for Alice's wedding.

Jimmy enjoyed the music as he played saxophone in the high school band. Willow had attended their last concert where he had been featured in a solo. Jimmy was going away to college in the fall as was Willow. He wanted to be an engineer; she had decided on a teaching career. She hoped to aspire to be like Miss Tyler, her fifth grade teacher who had encouraged her in elementary school. Jimmy's school was out of state so they probably didn't have a future together and that was okay with Willow. Bobby Carson was there with a girl Willow didn't know. And one of the boys from the Jones family from down the road was there, too. Jeff Templeton was there with Susan Sands. Willow hadn't spoken to him since the fiasco at the football dance. As she watched the two of them, she thought they were indeed perfect for each other with their arrogant superficiality. For the life of them, neither Alice nor Willow could figure out just who Connie Brown's date was.

All in all, it was a pleasant evening and Willow even enjoyed the goodnight kiss at her back door.

The time went quickly. It seemed only yesterday they were freshman in the new high school, gazing and reading the number to every door they passed in order to find their classes, trying to appear as cool as freshmen can be. It seemed like such a puzzle when they began and now they knew every inch of the building that had attempted to educate them over the four years. Certainly much had been learned in and outside the classrooms. And here it was time to graduate and move on to the next phase of their lives.

For Alice, it would be easy. Well, at least in the decision making for her future. She and Frank would be married in June, settle down, raise a house full of kids. Yes, Alice's life was pretty well planned out for her...at least for now. Willow, however, was off to the university. The separation would be great. It was time to put aside all the childhood experiences and everything they had shared from the heartaches and trials to the secrets only girls whispered at sleepovers. Those things would become precious memories. Things that once seemed important would become less significant over the years and those things that were indeed important would remain important for the rest of their lives.

Sitting in one of the folding chairs set up for the event, Eve anticipated the graduation ceremonies which were able to be held outside thanks to a significant break in the weather. It was just too much for Grandma and Grandpa Cain to get around these days, but Aunt Flo was at Eve's side. Eve hadn't counted on this being quite as an emotional event as it had become in just the few minutes they'd been there.

"Hurry, Eve, or we'll miss the ceremony," Blanche Cain called from the bottom of the stairway.

"Coming, Mother," Eve answered as she struggled into the new pair of shoes purchased for such an occasion.

Eve was the first in her family to graduate high school and her senior year had been a whirlwind of excitement. And now in less than a month, the biggest thrill of her life would take place. She would become Mrs. Chuck Evans.

From her place in the graduation line, she found her family several rows back from the front. Guess they had arrived early enough to get good seats. Dad was so proud of her and Mom was, too, although she was less likely to say so. Sister Flo sat next to Mom. Flo had disappointed her parents by dropping out of high school and getting a job. Little brother Zach was sitting next to Dad. It would be his turn next to graduate in about four more years. Eve knew he was probably wishing he was somewhere else about now. And next to Zach was Chuck Evans! The sight of him was almost more than she could handle. He was so handsome and charming and he made her laugh. And in two more weeks they would be husband and wife.

"Do you, Eve Joanne Cain, take this man, Charles W. Evans to be your lawfully wedded husband?"

"I do."

She wanted to cry through the ceremony, but the happiness she felt was a more powerful emotion.

And then, Chuck, in his light blue suit and white shirt and tie, holding her hands and smiling at her was also saying, "I do."

She didn't remember much else about the ceremony other than cutting the cake at the church reception and then getting in Chuck's truck for the honeymoon trip which consisted of going twenty miles south to a lodge.

During their three day stay, they had hiked trails and eaten in a real restaurant and made memories neither would ever forget. Just now she recalled how he looked when he woke up that first morning they were together and how he opened his eyes when she lightly kissed his cheek and how he smothered her with his love and how easily she accepted it.

"Evie Joanne," he murmured, "I absolutely adore you. I've imagined, but I didn't know these feelings even existed."

She snuggled to his chest.

"My darling, this is just the first page in our story. There are more wonderful chapters to be written."

He caressed her hair and felt the softness of her body against his. He loved this moment and prayed the feeling would never cease. But he was Chuck, after all.

"I'm starving," he said as he threw back the covers. "Let's go get some breakfast!"

Eve smiled. How many times in the short years they were together had she heard him say those very words? He was always hungry.

And now Eve was left with a hunger that would never again be satisfied.

The band was playing the strains of *Pomp and Circumstance,* the graduates were beginning to move and Eve stretched in her seat to find Willow in the procession.

Oh, Chuck, our Willow is graduating high school. You would be so proud of her!

Eve found Willow in the confusion following the ceremony long enough to give her hugs and tell her not to be too late. And then Willow and Jimmy, Alice and Frank, Bobby and his girlfriend all left to do a little celebrating. It would be the last time they were all together as a group.

University campus was a beautiful place, a mixture of old and new with its timeless buildings and modern construction blended together in perfect harmony. The grounds were well-kept with trees and flower gardens and all in all, it was a pleasant place to learn. But it was not the same as home. Willow was homesick and yet was too far away to visit often. But here she sat on a park bench near the dorm at the end of her junior year with the latest letter from her mother falling limp in her hand. She stared off into space with thoughts of times long since passed. Scott sat beside her. Dear Scott.

Willow and Scott met a year ago at the end of her sophomore year when they had a class together. It was a late afternoon class and frequently they had gotten something to eat and talk afterwards. It was a comfortable relationship. They'd found several things they had in common. Scott was a very serious student, dedicated to his work in the chemistry lab.

"What did she say?" he questioned Willow about the letter she held in her hand.

Willow, gathering strength she didn't have after the end of term exams, sighed and looked at the letter again.

"She says they don't expect Grandma Cain to make it through the week."

"You have finished your last exam, haven't you?"

"One more to go," she said slowly. "It's history with Professor Frost."

"The only logical thing to do is to check with Professor Frost, explain the situation and ask if you could take the exam early."

Scott was short on emotion and long on logic. He continued.

"I could go with you but I'm right in the middle of an experiment. It would be inconvenient for me to leave right now. Not practical at all."

When he had asked her to marry him, she had told him she would. It had not been at all romantic, more like scheduling an insignificant event or a lab in the chemistry department. Several companies were interested in Scott's talents. He ranked near the top in his science classes and had published several articles in trade magazines. And now the plan was in place. When he decided where he would locate, then Willow would look for a teaching position in the same area. Money would probably never be an issue. Scott would always have a good paying job. He had told her she didn't even need to work after they were married because his salary would be sufficient. But she wanted to teach, even arithmetic or mathematics as they called it these days. She wanted to make a difference in some child's life. She wanted to be the one to give some child the hope and determination to succeed in life. What could be greater than that?

Scott would say that greater than that would be a contribution to the scientific world. She was aware of his answer. At any rate, it was decided. First Scott's job, then Willow's position and then the wedding. They, well actually Willow, had already looked at wedding invitations and cake designs.

Aside from his scientific ambitions, Scott was knowledgeable in just about everything else. He could tell you statistics from almost any sport, but was not interested in playing any of them. He was good looking with straight brown hair and blue eyes, tall and oddly enough had an athletic build. Thick glasses helped his poor eyesight and were often used as an excuse when Willow tried to include him in an athletic adventure. The most physical endeavor she could expect of him was a walk through campus...if his schedule permitted. Six o'clock promptly each morning saw him in the lab working on experiments; his class schedules were worked out with precise timing to allow him time for twelve noon lunch that lasted no more the 30 minutes and a 5:30 evening meal. There would be no variance in the schedule.

However, Friday evenings were reserved for Willow exclusively. Those usually consisted of a movie and a pizza. Now here there was room for some degree of variety. The movie varied depending on which documentary was being shown that night and pizza could change from pepperoni to sausage every other week. Even the amount of time for their conversations seemed regulated.

"You go ahead with your experiment," she told him. "I'll talk to Professor Frost and then make arrangements to go back home. It's okay. You don't need to be there."

Seemingly satisfied with that arrangement, Scott briefly kissed her and started towards the lab, a bevy of books tucked under one arm. She watched him walk away, folded the letter and put it in her purse and started for Professor Frost's office.

The drive from campus back home gave Willow time to reflect about her life with Grandma Cain like the times she took Willow to the park when she was little and pushed her on the swings there. And she never seemed to tire of listening to Willow go on and on about a variety of subjects. Grandma Cain always had time for Willow and was patient in teaching her to experiment in the kitchen or be creative making party favors or crafts. How many times had they shared cookie baking in Grandma Cain's kitchen? Yes, Grandma Cain was someone she felt would always be there for her and now that was about to be taken away. Tears dropped to the steering wheel and Willow was not ashamed of them. Each one was a treasure, a dear memory of Grandma Cain.

Willow made it just in time to hold Grandma Cain's hand and whisper words of comfort in her ear. It was both helpful and comforting to be home and lend support while the family made the arrangements and grieved. Grandpa hugged Willow for a very long time and sat and reminisced about the life he and Grandma had shared and Willow felt quieted by his words, hearing of the happiness her grandparents had known. Aunt Flo and Mother, although grieving, were still capable of making decisions. Not so with Uncle Zach. His mother's death had sent him over the edge once again as Sally tried desperately to hold things together for him.

Excusing herself and feeling the need to be comforted as well, Willow placed a telephone call to Scott.

"You've reached the residence of Scott Hall. Should you care to leave a message, do so now."

She was always taken aback by the technology Scott and his friends had developed. And the message always surprised her.

"Scott, this is Willow. I just wanted to let you know that my grandmother has passed away. Visitation is Monday evening from 6-8 pm. Services will be Tuesday afternoon at 2."

Here she paused, questioning whether or not she should say more about perhaps him coming down for the funeral service. But she decided against it. Tuesdays Scott met with his group working on a breakthrough for something or other.

"Just wanted you to know," she said and then hung up the receiver.

There was a certain feel about funeral homes...subdued lighting, everyone talking in hushed tones, tissues being frequently applied to the eyes, hugs and words of condolences offered freely, stories told about the deceased. Then there's the overwhelming fragrance of flowers sent by friends, neighbors, or organizations. Grandma and Grandpa Cain were well-known in the community and had done a lot of church volunteering so there were numerous amounts of people there, some Willow knew well or others she had never seen before or hadn't seen for quite some time.

Grandpa Cain mostly sat in one of the chairs to rest his aging body, but would frequently stand to greet people, especially old buddies from the war who he slapped on the back and swapped stories with. It seemed like a reunion of sorts and Willow pondered why there weren't meetings like this during happier occasions other than funerals. Mom and Aunt Flo stood and greeted people as they came in. Sally was there but Uncle Zach was nowhere around.

A very tiny girl approached Willow. Although there was something familiar about her, Willow couldn't really place who she was until she spoke.

"I'm Jane Jones. My family was neighbors to yours when we were growing up."

"Of course," Willow recognized the little girl she had walked home from school with so many times. "It's been at least three or four years since I've seen you. How are you?"

She grabbed the fragile body and hugged her.

"I'm fine," Jane said. "I'll be graduating next year. I saw where your grandmother passed and I wanted to come. You were always so kind to me. And I will never forget the Christmas you and your mother brought some things to our house."

Both girls stood there with tears in their eyes for two entirely different reasons.

Willow hugged Jane again.

"I'm so glad you came, Jane. Thank you."

Alice was there with Frank, pregnant again with child number three. Although they wrote sometimes, both girls had been busy...Willow with school and obviously Alice with her family. Willow had a strange feeling when she saw Alice and Frank together. They appeared so happy and Alice was fulfilling her dream. What of Willow's dreams? It seemed her dreams were lagging behind everyone else's dreams. And some days she wasn't even sure what her dreams really were anymore. Perhaps she really needed some time off from the daily grind of college.

"You look really good, Willow," Alice had said.

"Thanks. You, too. I see you're working on number three."

Alice always had a beautiful glow about her when she was pregnant. She laughed.

"Frank says at least three more, but I don't know."

There was no doubt in Willow's mind that there would be more children if possible. Frank and Alice made great parents.

"You make a great mom, Alice. You have everything you've ever wanted."

"Yes," she answered. "All I ever wanted was to marry Frank and have his kids. And you? How about you, Willow? Anyone in your life?"

Willow blushed a bit.

"Well, yes. His name is Scott. He's a chemist."

"Eew!" Alice reacted. "Sounds pretty boring to me."

Willow frowned at that remark.

Alice continued.

"Serious? Any wedding plans?"

"Oh, yes," Willow replied. "After graduation. One more year. Doesn't seem possible."

"You'll be having kids of your own soon then."

"If they're on the schedule."

Alice gave a bewildered look at that statement, having no clue as to what it meant. Willow laughed a bit and then tried to cover up her embarrassment at how ridiculous that sounded.

"Oh, look," Alice pointed out. "There's Bobby Carson. You remember him, don't you?"

"Sure. Haven't seen him in ages, probably since we graduated high school."

Willow looked in the direction of Alice's gesture.

"Excuse me. I need to greet him. He looks lost. And, Alice, congratulations on this baby."

He had changed. Bobby Carson was even taller than Willow had remembered. There were still freckles on his face, but they seemed to give him a distinguished look now and his brown hair was combed up in a curl at the front. Certainly his shoulders were broader than she recalled. But the moment he saw her, his green eyes began to dance. He held out his hands and she took them.

"So good of you to come," she offered.

"It's been a while," they both said, speaking over each other.

They both laughed at that.

"I'm sorry about your grandmother," he said quietly. "That's got to be rough, you being away at school and all."

"Yes," she admitted and realized how much she missed the compassion she felt from him right now.

"You look real good."

"Thanks," she responded. "You, too. You've grown up."

She laughed uncomfortably at herself this time at how ridiculous her statement sounded.

"Well, whatever you've been doing," he continued, "it certainly seems to have agreed with you. You are just as beautiful as I remembered."

Now things *were* uncomfortable.

"I just saw Alice over there," Willow attempted to change the subject.

He looked and then turned back to Willow.

"Wow," he said. "Pregnant again. Wow."

Time to change the subject again, Willow thought.

"So, what's been happening with you?"

"Not a whole lot. I own my own auto shop now. Even have one employee," he said proudly. "That's one other than myself," he clarified.

"That's great. I always knew you'd be a success."

"Well, I don't know about success…it's a lot of work and I put in some long hours."

"But it's something you like."

"Oh, yeah, but there's more to life than all work. I like to fish and I play baseball a couple of nights a week in season."

"Not married yet?" she said boldly, and again laughed at herself.

He laughed, too.

"Oh, no, still lookin' for just the right one. You?"

Suddenly she blushed and she knew she was blushing and she knew he knew she was blushing.

"Nothing serious," she denied.

"Yeah. *Don't settle for less than you really want,*" he said.

"Grandma Bessie?"

"Yeah, Grandma Bessie."

They both laughed. How long had it been since she'd thought about Grandma Bessie's wise advice?

"Hey, how long are you goin' to stay around?" he asked.

"Not going back 'til Sunday. Exams are over with so I'm taking a few days here at the beginning of the summer."

"You're gonna be tired after the funeral on Tuesday, so how about I pick you up on Wednesday and we'll go get some breakfast?"

"Oh, sure," she hesitated. "But I thought you had a business to run."

"Didn't I tell you I hired an employee?" he grinned. "That's the nice thing about being the boss."

He was prompt as she knew he would be. She was dressed casually in red peddle pushers and a red and white checked shirt. As he opened the door of his pickup for her, she noticed how tan he was already at the beginning of the summer and how muscular his forearms were. His whole manner was light and carefree and she relaxed as she watched him walk around the truck to get into the driver's seat.

"So where are we going?" she asked.

"There's a little café not far from here if that's okay with you," he replied.

She smiled when she realized that the plan could be altered. As a matter of fact, she kind of felt giddy at the prospect of something loosely planned. What a refreshing change!

It was indeed a small café with black and white tile on the floor and red vinyl seat coverings, nothing elegant with a touch of nostalgia. Even music selectors at the tables.

"Is this okay?" he asked.

When had Scott ever asked her opinion? It was always the same booth at the same pizza place preceded by the same row in the same movie theatre every Friday night.

"This is great," she said as he situated himself across from her in the booth. "You come here often?"

"Once in a while. They have okay food. Besides is saves me from cooking."

"As I recall, you were a pretty good cook. At least you get into your work if I remember correctly…"

He pretended he didn't know what she was talking about.

"You know…the day I brought the persimmon pudding and you were making dumplings or something and had flour all over your…your apron."

She waited to see if that had offended him.

"Oh, yeah, I remember that. You stayed and helped out."

He paused, pleased she had remembered that day, too.

"Guess that's one of the times you weren't upset about some remarks Connie Brown made."

Oh, oh! He got her back with that comment.

"I still get upset when I think about her and how nasty she was to me. Saying I was named after a tree and said I cried like a *weeping willow.*

"That's one reason why I brought you here," he looked intently into her eyes.

"What?" she questioned.

"Don't look now, but when you have a chance, check out the waitress with the bleached hair."

Willow discreetly turned and immediately found the bleached hair, gathered in a hair net. Gobs of makeup painted her face. An apron was tied around her bulging middle.

"Is that?"

He shook his head.

"But that doesn't look at all like…" her words drifted.

"It is. I thought you might be interested."

"But how? What happened? She told everyone all about how she was going to college to be this huge success and…"

"She did go to college. Lasted about a semester. Came back here looking haggard and tired and then she started gaining weight and then there was this baby."

He paused and Willow looked shocked.

"Needless to say, her parents weren't pleased and I understand they kicked her out. Anyway, she's been working at this diner now for more than a year."

"Oh, Bobby, that's so sad. I feel sorry for her."

"What?" he gasped. "You've cried on my shoulder a dozen times over things that girl did to you and said about you. And now you feel sorry for her after everything she's done to you?"

She looked at him with wide eyes.

"And I'd expect nothing less of you, Willow Evans," he smiled, picking up the menu with one hand as Connie approached the table with her order pad in hand.

"Hey, Bobby, what'll yah have?"

"I'll have the special, Connie," he said, closing the menu and looking straight at Willow.

"And you, ma'am?"

"Hello, Connie."

"My gosh! If it isn't Willow Evans!" Connie burst forth. "I heard about your grandma. Sorry."

"Thanks," Willow said in return. "It's good to see you, Connie. I'll have the special, too. Suddenly I'm really hungry."

Connie sashayed back to the grill to place the order and Willow continued their conversation.

"I can't believe it. That is so bizarre! She was going to be soooo successful!"

"*Failure is success we learn from,*" he reminded her.

She didn't have to ask. She recognized it as more of Grandma Bessie's wisdom.

"Stuff happens," he replied. "When we were kids we never knew how our lives would turn out. Wonder if our teachers in grade school ever thought about what we'd become."

"Yeah," she smiled. "Students like Bucky Wilson?"

"Believe it or not, he works for a lumber yard and does a pretty good job of it. Shows up for work and is dependable."

"No kidding!" she was surprised. "Well, I am glad for that, too. It took me a long time to forgive him for making us lose our arithmetic homework and for messing up your bike."

"He was a mess all right. Funny how people can change."

Connie returned with their breakfasts, asking if there was anything else she could bring them while she chomped away on a piece of gum. Satisfied they were good for now, she pulled her pencil from behind her ear and went on to another customer waiting to order.

"That is so weird. Not in a million years would I have thought Connie Brown would end up waitressing in a diner."

She chewed on a piece of bacon and could not believe how good it tasted. Having breakfast here was a really good idea.

"Where are your little brother and sister now?" Willow asked.

"Beth is a senior this year. Pretty as a picture, even though she is my sister. I'm sending her to college. She's gonna have no choice. I want her to make something of herself."

"I knew she would be a beauty. She was always a cute girl. *You're* sending her to college?"

"Yeah, Pop doesn't think it's all that important, but she's smart and I think she deserves it."

"You deserved it, too. You were always smart in school. Helped me a bunch in arithmetic."

"I did okay," he said. "But I like what I'm doing now. I've taken a few automotive classes and I'm at peace with that. Please tell me you do better at arithmetic these days."

She laughed.

"Well, I can balance my checkbook now. The bank is real proud of me."

Her eyes danced as she joked with him and he noticed the way she had of tipping her head one direction when she did.

He really did seem to be at peace with what he'd chosen in life. Why did she think the look on his face was asking her if she was at peace with the decisions she'd made?

Bobby continued.

"My little brother is a sophomore. Plays football. Likes girls. And a lot of girls like him. The phone's always tied up with his calls. Works for me some."

"So you got a lot of business?"

"Yep. A couple of big accounts. As a matter of fact, I have a contract to work on the cars for the police department. That's a pretty good amount of work. May even have to hire someone else to help out."

Willow studied Bobby's face. It was alive when he talked about work or sending his little sister to college. That kind of enthusiasm was something she hadn't witnessed for a long time.

Willow couldn't remember when breakfast had tasted this good. He watched her eat with relish and assumed she surely must have been as hungry as she had said. Then suddenly Willow approached Bobby about something she carried constantly with her these days.

"Bobby," she began, "you remember all the things about my Dad's death?"

He stopped eating, wiped his mouth and looked intently at her.

"I don't know much except what little you said and what was rumored around."

"Well, I've been thinking. I have a lot of unanswered questions surrounding his death. I think I'd like to do some searching."

He picked up his fork again and seemed to be lost in his eating for a time.

"You want me to help you in some way?"

"Well, I guess I value your opinion. My Mom told me that the report said he was going too fast and missed a corner out on a country road. But there was a note…a suicide note. Something just doesn't feel quite right. I think there may have been more to it than that."

He thought for a time and then took another sip of coffee.

"What I think, Willow," he said with a look of seriousness, "is if you have concerns, if you have doubts, you need to find solutions and put it to rest."

He paused.

"Of course, with that said, you'd also have to accept what you find out to be true."

He was right, of course. Something she hadn't really thought about…that her findings might not be what she wanted to hear.

"Tell you what," he said, wiping his face on the napkin and laying down his fork. "I'll do some asking around. The guys on the force often come by and shoot the breeze. Let me see what I can find out."

Another pause.

"And I will be discreet," he said as if it had been decided. He continued his breakfast, taking time to notice the look in Willow's eyes.

"I would appreciate that very much," she replied.

"It's settled then," she said. "I've decided."

"But it's not in the plan, Willow. The whole idea of making a plan is to see it through."

"Well, I guess some plans are made to be changed. At least this one. I've decided to go back home for the summer. One last summer at home before launching into my senior year of college."

She suddenly realized that circumstances surrounding her father's death was something she had never discussed with Scott. Sitting on a bench in the middle of campus was a lot different than sitting in a café with an old school chum.

"I will have to think about this," Scott was clearly frustrated. "A change of this magnitude, Willow, can upset other things. It's a domino effect, you know."

"No, Scott," Willow was firm. "You don't have to labor over thinking about this. I've already decided. I need to resolve some things before I can continue my own life. You have your lab work here for the summer. And I intend to return for the fall semester. Don't worry, Scott, I'm entirely capable of handling this on my own."

"But what about our Friday nights?" he was grasping at straws.

"I'm sure Friday nights can come and go without me. And if your schedule permits, we'll see about that next fall."

He sat staring after her as she walked away. How could this be happening? Willow must have lost her mind. This was indeed disrupting the schedule.

Chapter Eight

He dialed the number she had written on the napkin. His hands were sweaty and his heart was beating so fast, his chest heaved. It rang three times. Maybe she wasn't home or maybe his timing was bad or maybe…

"Hello."

"Willow?" he asked.

"Who's calling, please?"

"It's me, Willow. It's Bobby Carson."

Her tone of voice changed.

"Oh, hi, Bobby. I didn't recognize your voice."

"Yeah…er…uh…" he stammered. "I have a piece of news I think you'll be interested in."

"About my Dad?"

"Yeah, about that situation. I guess it could wait 'til you got back, but I wanted you to know."

Actually, he just wanted to hear her voice and feel the excitement she produced in him.

"Good. I'm leaving here tomorrow afternoon. I can't wait to start working on this."

"Okay. Call me when you get in."

Bobby couldn't wait either. He couldn't wait to see Willow again.

The open for business sign had been out since 6 am when he'd come down to the garage to open up. Jeb was already changing the oil in Mr. Peterson's Ford pickup. There was the sound of the lift going up and down and Jeb's voice singing along with the radio that was blaring from its spot on the top shelf. Bobby Carson sat in his office, shuffling papers across his desk. She hadn't called. He had stayed up late last night thinking she would call. It didn't make much difference that he had stayed up because he couldn't sleep anyway. But she hadn't called.

He leaned back in his tilt chair, stretching his legs up to rest them on the desk, putting his arms over his head and closed his eyes. It was the same as it had been all night long. Every time he closed his eyes, all he could see was her eyes.

"Well, is this how the boss works?"

He opened his eyes as his chair came to rest with a thud. He drank in the picture before him. She stood in the doorway wearing white shorts with a print blouse tied at the waist. Her hair was damp from the shower as its curly ringlets began to tighten as it dried. Her lips were pink and oh, her lips. He couldn't look any longer if he was to keep his composure.

"What's the matter?" she laughed. "Caught the boss loafing?"

He jumped to his feet and cleaning off a chair, motioned for her to sit, trying to reclaim his voice.

"I thought you'd call last night," he blurted out.

That was dumb, he thought.

"I didn't get in 'til late," she smiled, realizing his discomfort. "There was a lot of rain east of here so I had to drive slow."

"Glad you did," he said, once again sitting down in his tilt chair. "Want you to be safe."

And at that point she knew he really meant it and was thinking of her well-being.

"I'm really excited about the prospect of finding out some information," she prodded.

"Yes. Okay. I told you that the police come in here regularly for work on their vehicles. Well, Tim O'Toole was in here a couple of days ago. He's a relatively new detective on the force and I was asking him some questions. He seemed interested in helping out. He's a young officer but interested in what they call cold cases. I told him I would bring you around sometime and arrange a meeting between the two of you."

That seemed to please her and he was relieved. She made no effort to leave; and since he had used up all the information he had for her, he sat awkwardly.

"Thank you," she said softly. "You want to show me around this place?"

He got up and held the door for her; and as she passed by him, he smelled her perfume and it made him weak. She was innocent and he liked that. She asked questions about things she saw in the garage and he was more than happy to explain them to her. As they finished the tour, she looked up at him.

"So when do you think I can meet with Tim O'Toole?"

"He's coming over in the morning to bring one of the cars. I'll call you when he comes in."

"Sounds good to me."

With that she left and he felt foolish, like he should have complimented her on her hair or something, like he should have said more, possibly made plans with her to do something fun. But he would see her again tomorrow for sure and besides, he was busy pitching in the baseball game tonight.

He was in the sixth inning before he saw her, sitting there in the stands, her curly hair catching the last rays of the evening sun. She had come to the baseball game. Why had she come to the baseball game? Had she come to see him? Probably not. Possibly she just liked baseball. His thoughts cost him a batter to walk. He needed to concentrate on his game.

Her reason for being there was pretty clear by the end of the ninth when she made her way down to the dugout and stood nearby until he came over the fence.

"Thought I'd come down and scout out the local talent," she smiled.

"Find any?"

"Um," she pretended to think. "The pitcher for the red team was pretty fair. Maybe easily distracted."

So she had noticed how he gave up the walk. She *had* been paying attention.

"I thought I'd like to get a hamburger and maybe you'd like to come with me," she ventured.

A couple of players from his team passed by and turned to give him a questioning look when they saw the young lady he apparently knew.

"Sure," he was both surprised and pleased. "Sure, okay. Just let me change a bit. I'll meet you at the truck in the parking lot."

"Okay," she smiled and he weakened again.

"You know which one it is, don't you?" he turned as he started to walk away.

"I think I can find it."

On his way to the truck, he thought surely it must have been a dream...her coming to talk with him and then asking him to get something to eat with her. Maybe he would go to his truck and she wouldn't be there at all. But when his truck came into view, she was standing there, leaning against it. She was still in the white shorts with the blouse tied up as she had been that morning. Good, he thought. She looked fantastic in those shorts.

She leaned against the truck waiting for Bobby to come out of the park. Perhaps she'd been a bit forward in asking him to go for hamburgers. But they were friends, after all. Had been since they were little kids. And then when she saw him coming across the parking lot, duffle bag slung over one shoulder, she was sure she had made the right decision. He was in jeans and a white tee shirt which neatly formed around his chest and arms. As he walked straight towards her, she became a little short of breath.

"Hello," he said as he approached.

"Hello, yourself." she responded. "You hungry?"

"Starved. You got any place in mind?"

She smiled.

"You drive and let's just see what we can find."

She liked that...his willingness to just let things happen. He drove the strip and when the A & W root beer stand came into view, they both said at the same time that this was the place. How different this was from the well-thought-out plans with Scott. And wouldn't he be shook up to do something this spontaneous? Scott would have really been thrown off guard by what else happened that evening. After the A & W scene, they stopped by to pick up swim suits and went down to the lake for an early summer swim. Although the water was cool, neither Bobby nor Willow seemed to mind. You couldn't hear the splashing over the laughter.

The ringing of the telephone woke her up the next morning.

"Willow, Tim O'Toole is right here at the garage and has a few minutes to talk with you."

"I'll be right there."

She arrived in blue capris with a light blue and yellow flowered shirt. She wore white sandals and came equipped with notebook and pen. How could she possibly look that good after an evening of swimming at the lake? After the introductions, Bobby showed them to the room he called his office and closed the door behind him as he left. He frequently looked through the glass window in the office door to see that everything was going okay. Or was it just the chance to look once more into her face?

"How can I help you?" Tim O'Toole was saying. "Bobby has told me a little bit about what you might be looking for…re-opening a cold case?"

Tim O'Toole was not a local boy. He was terribly handsome with his black hair and steel blue eyes. When he smiled, it was hard to concentrate on the issue at hand.

"Yes," she faltered. "My father was killed in a car crash in 1942. It was ruled a suicide. Apparently there was a suicide note left. From what I gather from my mother, there was no cause for him to feel that way. I realize that things can happen to alter people, but I do not think my father was a candidate for suicide."

She saw the look in his face. Perhaps he didn't believe her. She needed to convince him this was worth looking into; but the more she said, the worse the picture seemed to be. A man going off to the service, having some last drinks with his buddies before he left. Impaired driving certainly was not out of the question. But then the suicide note?

"I'll see what I can find out. I have his name and the date. I'll find out who the officer on duty was. Perhaps you could check the newspapers for what was published," he said as he stood to leave. "Then we'll get together again and go over the information we've uncovered."

He fumbled in his shirt pocket and produced a card with his name on it and told her to call him if she found any information. She tucked the card inside her purse.

Willow paid a visit to the local library that afternoon; and with the help of the library staff was able to locate the newspapers for May 15, 1942. At first, she scanned the articles for new information. The second time through them, she read for detail. She inquired about making copies of the three newspaper articles concerning the accident as well as the obituary. After the librarian made the copies and she had paid for them, Willow left the library and headed over to visit with Grandpa George.

He was sitting on the front porch and was happy to see his favorite and only grandchild.

"Come sit a spell," he said, gesturing towards one of the wicker rockers that had occupied the front porch for as long as she could remember.

"Okay, Grandpa," she sighed, as she sat down.

"So what's my girl up to today?" he asked, peering at her over his glasses.

"Grandpa," she began, "I don't want to upset you, but I would like to ask you some questions…about my Dad."

He nodded his head and she was pleased to see he was not opposed to talking about the subject.

"Tell me everything you remember about him, please, Grandpa," she begged.

Looking into her eyes and seeing so much of Chuck in her, he began.

"Well, I always liked your Dad…right from the very beginning. And I never saw your Mom so happy as when she was with him. When you looked at them together, you just knew something was right between them. And I never saw that disappear. I'm quite sure they loved each other like no other.

Now, he was a good worker, but he loved to have fun. Good lookin' guy. His hair was the color of yours and curly like yours, too. And you have his same eyes. Many's the time your Grandma and I made comment on that.

But I suspect you want to know about the accident. Awful. Just awful. Never encountered anything that got to me more..."

A cloud had come over his face as he recalled the incident.

"Called in the middle of the night. Your Mom was crying so hard she could hardly talk. Grandma went to take care of you and I took your Mom to identify him. Worst thing I've ever had to do in my life."

Tears slid down his cheeks and Willow questioned her wisdom in coming here, especially because of Grandma Cain's recent death. She gently put her hand over on his arm.

It was what she wanted to hear. Someone else who shared her thoughts.

"Thanks, you've been a big help. How about comin' over to the house for supper tonight, Grandpa?" she concluded. "Mom and I would be glad to have you."

"Jest might do that, Missy," he waved to her as she started down the porch steps. "Yep, tell your Mom I'll be there...with my appetite."

Eve was bit edgy about having Willow prying into the past. Although she, too, had wanted answers, the accident had happened a long time ago and maybe reviving it might cause more hurt. Especially Willow's latest scheme.

"I know how you feel, Mom, but I swear I won't upset them. I'm just looking for information. Trust me."

Eve had relented, giving her all the information she could remember about Chuck's parents. Eve hadn't had any contact with them since they had left town. They moved to Graceville shortly after the accident. And their names were Charles and

Nancy Evans. And more importantly, they wanted nothing to do with Eve or Willow.

Graceville wasn't that big of a town. A couple of grocery stores, a bank, some fast food places, several churches and gas stations and an assortment of middle class houses. After Willow drove the main street of town, she spotted a telephone booth and pulled over. Sure enough, a tattered phone book hung from a chain inside the booth. She fumbled through the pages until she came to the name Evans. Adele couldn't be the one and Adam either. She quickly copied down street addresses and numbers for the other two. She started with the most likely...Charles Evans; and putting her dime in the coin slot, began to dial the number listed. Her heart raced as she heard the ring of the phone. *Please answer,* she spoke out loud.

"Hello," a woman's voice answered.

"Hello," Willow returned. "I'm trying to contact a Charles or Nancy Evans."

"You got the wrong number," came the reply.

"Wait," she started, "do you know anyone by that name?"

But it was too late. The woman had hung up the receiver. Willow fumbled for another dime; and once again inserting the coin, she carefully dialed the next number.

This time a man answered on the second ring.

"Evans' residence."

"Hello, I'm trying to contact a Charles or Nancy Evans."

"Yeah, what is this about?"

"It's about your son, Chuck. Did you have a son by that name?"

There was silence on the other end of the line.

"Please, sir..."

"You have the wrong number."

A click of the receiver ended the phone call.

Willow was excited. No, she didn't have the wrong number. The man who had just hung up the phone *was* her grandfather. She was sure of it. But she was also sure of the reception she would get should she go to the house. But her curiosity was running wild so she got directions from an attendant at one of the gas stations and drove to the address listed in the phone book. She parked discreetly across the street from the little house painted blue with white shutters. Then, a stroke of luck. A gentleman opened the front door of the house and made his way to the street to a mailbox. He was tall and thin and his hair matched Willow's in color. A feeling came over her. This indeed surely was her grandfather.

She shared the news with Eve that evening and again she was delving into photos. Eve had made the trip to the attic to retrieve the photo album from the trunk. Willow made her way through the photos; and when she came to the one of her with her paternal grandparents, she was sure the man walking to the mailbox was indeed the same man in the photograph. It was too much for Eve to read through the newspaper articles so Willow kept those to herself. But she had another question to ask.

"Mom, do you know who Dad was with that night? Celebrating with friends before they went into the service? Who were these friends?"

"The same ones in the photo," Eve remembered as she found the photo in the album once again. "This is Hank Roberston and Jerry Wells and your Dad and Stace Grant."

"Are they still around?"

"Well after that night, Jerry went overseas and was killed in the war. Hank Robertson went to the service and came back and moved to East Town the last I heard and Stace Grant still lives here somewhere out in the country."

"But Hank and Stace went to the war?"

"No, actually Hank did, but Stace was rejected. He didn't go, but he was celebrating with them that night."

"Thanks, Mom," Willow said as she kissed her mother and tried to make the rest of the evening pleasant, although ideas surrounding the accident continued to swirl in her head.

He hadn't seen her in two days and it seemed like two weeks. Maybe he should call her. Maybe she was busy. No, he needed to just hang loose a bit. At any rate, Clyde Riggs wouldn't care about those things. He would only care about his '52 Ford being serviced and ready for pick up by 4 o'clock this afternoon. Bobby ducked once more under the hood of the car.

"Hello," she announced her arrival at the garage.

Bobby almost dropped the wrench he was holding and stood up from under the hood of a '53 Dodge, banging his head in the process. He took in the entire picture from her tennis shoes and jeans right down to her oversized shirt as he rubbed his aching skull.

"Oh, hi," he tried not to show how nervous he was. "Haven't seen you around much. I was wondering if you had gotten a job on the police force or whatever."

She smiled and rose to his challenge.

"Not yet, but Tim and I are meeting later this afternoon so he may be ready to offer me a job."

He wiped his hands on a towel and came over to talk to her.

"How's it going?"

"Slow. I've gotten the newspaper articles and I went to see my grandparents in Graceville."

He raised his eyebrows.

"No, I didn't actually talk to them, but I did speak with Grandpa on the phone and I saw him come out of the house to get the mail."

"Wow, you're really becoming quite the detective. I'm impressed."

"A long way yet to go. I have the names now of the guys who were with him that night. Two of them live not far from here and are still alive."

She dug in the pocket of her jeans and pulled out a piece of paper and read from it.

"So now I'll be looking for Hank Robertson and Stace Grant."

Bobby thought a minute.

"I don't know anything about a Hank Robertson, but I might be able to help you with Stace Grant. He comes in here once in a while and hangs out some."

"Really?" she was interested. "Maybe you could set it up so I could talk to him?"

"I'll see what I can do."

She touched his arm.

"I know it's not your problem, so if you don't want to get involved, I'll understand."

He reacted strongly to her touch.

"Now, who said I didn't want to be involved?"

She stood there thinking there should be more to be said. She dug her hands in her pockets not willing to walk away just yet.

"You comin' to my game tonight?" he blurted out. "I mean, I'd like for you to come…if you want to. We could go somewhere after if you want."

"Sounds good to me," she replied, ignoring his awkwardness. "I'll see you there."

The game was called at the seventh inning because of rain. He found her waiting for him under the bleachers close again to where the players came from the locker room. She had changed from the jeans to shorts again and she took his breath away the minute he saw her. After greeting, they stood watching the rain come down in torrents.

"I think we'd better wait a few minutes," he said. "This is comin' down pretty hard."

She agreed and noticed he was once again in jeans and a white tee shirt.

"How'd your meeting come out with Tim?" he asked.

"Oh, slight progress, I guess," she jolted herself from the thoughts that kept emerging without any warning.

"Uh, he found the files and hadn't had the time to go over them thoroughly yet. He glanced through my newspaper clippings and nothing jumped out at him. Thought it was a good idea to perhaps contact the two men who were with him at the bar."

"Okay. Sounds like a plan. Stace Grant hasn't been in for a while so he's about due to come by. Hey, rain's slacking off some. You want me to drive the truck up for you?"

"No, I won't melt. I'll just follow you."

She slipped off her shoes and together they splashed through puddles. She struggled to keep up with him. He reached the truck first; and opening the door, he grabbed her arm to help her up in the truck. By the time he reached the driver's side, he was drenched. He reached in back for a towel and offered it to her. He watched as she rubbed it over her head and arms and noticed how her curly hair only curled all the more with the moisture. Why had he never noticed that about her before? He quickly ran the towel over his own face and arms.

"You got any ideas for tonight?" he asked her.

"You don't have anything planned?" she was shocked at herself for saying that.

He looked surprised.

"Should I have given this more thought? I thought we could decide together what we might do."

She was struck by his entire manner, his easygoing way of tackling life.

"Okay," she said. "You hungry?"

"Always hungry!" he said with gusto.

"Maybe we could pick up a pizza or something," she suggested.

"I like pizza," he concurred. "How about we take it back to my place? Maybe watch a movie or something."

"I'd like that," she smiled. "But…your place? Your Dad's place?"

"Oh, it's okay. Dad is gone for the evening and so is Beth and my little brother is staying over at a friend's house."

She relaxed a bit at that news. She relaxed even more sitting next to him on the sofa, their feet propped up on the same ottoman, mouthfuls of pizza…pizza with the works on it, not just pepperoni or sausage…and glasses of soda in their hands and some kind of movie playing on the television. She thought once that she should probably tell him about Scott, but that thought quickly vanished; and when he put his arm around her shoulder, it just felt so comfortable that she decided now was not the time.

It was twenty miles to East Town and that would give her plenty of time to prepare her thoughts for meeting Hank Robertson, but somehow her thoughts kept making the journey back to last night and sitting on the sofa with Bobby and how comforting it felt for him to have his arm around her.

Chapter Nine

She couldn't find any phone booths in East Town. It wasn't even as big as Graceville had been. Well, that should make it easier to find Hank Robertson. She pulled into the parking lot of a little café, sat at the counter and ordered a soft drink. The waitress didn't know Hank Robertson but returned a few minutes later from the kitchen with the cook. If anyone would know Hank Robertson, it would be him. He was a man of about fifty years old and claimed he knew everyone in East Town. But he shook his head when Willow gave him the name.

"You sure he's in East Town?" he said, seemingly puzzled.

"That's what I understand," she answered. "Possibly somewhere in his early to mid-40's or so."

The cook continued to shake his head and Willow thanked him and turned to leave.

"Wait. Wait, Miss," the cook flung his arm after her. "I know who you you're talkin' about. Old Henry. Henry Robertson. The *Hank* threw me for a minute. Nobody calls him *Hank* around here. Well, here's his address."

He quickly wrote some words on a paper napkin and then handed it to her with a smile as well as some sketchy verbal directions.

"Thank you so much," Willow smiled back. "You've been a big help."

Again, hope filled Willow's heart. Now if only she remembered the directions correctly. She drove to the second stop sign and turned right. She was concerned because she felt like she was leaving the town. Perhaps she had not remembered the directions correctly. Checking the address again, she began to look for Washington Street. She was sure the man at the restaurant had said that Washington Street only went to the left. And there it was! She maneuvered the car into a left turn and began to look for the house number. Houses were farther apart here. 32327. She repeated the number in her mind. There was 32323 and then she was there. A ranch style house was nestled in a grove of trees at the end of a rather long lane flanked by white fencing. She brought the car to a stop right in front of the door. A knock on the door brought a response from a rather plain looking woman with a friendly face.

“”Yes?” she asked as she opened the door.

“Hello. My name is Willow Evans and I’m looking for a man by the name of Hank Robertson.”

Without question, she invited Willow inside.

“Henry’s out back. Come this way.”

And she led the way to the back patio where a tall, lanky man was planting flowers. As he stood up straight and turned towards her, she was convinced this was the same man from the photo.

“Henry, there’s someone here to see you.”

Henry stood and stared into Willow’s face with a look that reflected the alarm he felt inside.

“What was your name again, dear?” the woman asked, touching Willow’s arm.

“I think I can guess,” Hank said slowly. “You’re Chuck Evans’ girl, aren’t you?”

“Why, yes, how did you know?”

“The eyes…the hair. Something I’ll never forget.”

He seemed stunned, like he had seen a ghost from his past. Finally, he came to himself and offered Willow a seat.

“Mary, bring us some lemonade,” he said to his wife and she left quietly for the kitchen.

“I always thought some day you might come,” he said simply.

“As you probably can guess,” Willow began, “I have some unanswered questions about my Dad.”

“There’s a lot of him in you,” he stated, still overcome by her presence.

"Thank you. I think that's a compliment. I guess you knew my Dad pretty well."

"Yes, I did. We all went to high school together. And we were all headed to the war together."

A cloud seemed to descend over him as he remembered and Willow waited patiently. The arrival of the lemonade seemed to bring him back to the conversation. Mary delivered the lemonade and discreetly made an exit back to the house.

"My questions are about the night of the accident," she continued. "Can you tell me what you remember about that night?"

He thought for a few moments; and then with a sigh, he delved into memories that were still vivid to him.

"We were all gonna be shipped out. Well, all except Stace. He was rejected, but Chuck said it was ok for him to come along. Anyway, Jerry decided we should all get together for one last blow out. You know, a little drinking and laughing and joking. And that's what we did. At that time, I didn't know that Jerry and I would be the only two going…and I'd be the only one coming back."

He stopped here with emotion. Willow sat quietly until he was ready to continue. After a few minutes, he found the words.

"It really wasn't that late when we broke up. Your Dad wanted to get back home to Eve and he wasn't much of a drinker anyway, so he was the first to leave. Then Stace Grant. Jerry and I stayed a little longer, mostly because there were these two girls there who had caught our interest. Anyway, Chuck left and then Stace and the next thing I knew Stace was back, saying there'd been an accident and we needed to come quick. By the time we got there, the police were there and a wrecker had been called. The car was a mess…all smashed up and…are you sure you want to hear all of this?"

She nodded.

"His head had hit the windshield and there was no way he could have survived the crash. No way. I'm tellin' you, that sobered all of us up real quick."

"I believe there was something about a suicide note?" Willow asked.

Again Hank looked puzzled.

"Yeah, Stace was the one who found it. He was down at the site actually helping to pull the car up. Strange. Chuck was fine when he left the bar. Sad about leaving you and your mom to go to the war, but not depressed or anything. Least not that I could tell. But yet there was the note signed and all."

Willow sipped the lemonade so the throat that had constricted would relax. Sitting the glass aside, she asked again.

"Is there anything else you can tell me?"

"That's about it. I shipped out the day after the funeral. Never have seen anybody since then. Of course, Jerry didn't make it back."

"You do not keep in touch with Stace Grant?"

"Nope. He was always kind of an outsider, but your dad must have felt sorry for him or something, 'cause he always included him."

Willow stood to leave.

"Thank you," she said and then offered a hug to the man she'd just met.

Somehow they shared something in common.

"You have his hair and eyes, you know," Hank murmured.

A chill swept through Willow's body.

"So I've been told."

Her mind raced on the drive back to the city. She needed to find Stace Grant and get his side of the story. He would know more details if he was the one who had been right there at the accident.

"Three phone calls, Willow," Eve said. "You're just the most popular young lady. What do you think I am, your personal secretary?"

She smiled, teasing Willow with her statements. She loved having Willow home for the summer and fully realized that things would change again after college graduation. They just needed to make the most of the time they were allowed to be together. She'd only met Scott once and he appeared to be a nice enough guy, but she saw no chemistry going on between Scott and Willow. She smiled at that recollection and the use of the term *chemistry* since Scott was a chemist. But she hadn't said anything to Willow. Perhaps this summer away from each other would make a difference in Willow and Scott's relationship.

Willow took the messages. She would call Scott first. Recalling his schedule, she thought this would be a good time to call.

"No, Scott, I am not coming back for a while," she said, appearing to be annoyed with him. "I have not finished what I intended to accomplish this summer, but I am working on it. Oh, sure, I know you have a meeting today in fifteen minutes. That's why I called you back now."

She hung up the receiver and sat staring for a few minutes. It had not been a comforting telephone call.

Tim O'Toole was next on her list. She dialed the number…the one he had left with her in case she needed to talk to him.

"It's Willow Evans," she said.

"Good. I was hoping it would be you."

"Well, that's good 'cause it's me."

He laughed.

"I thought perhaps it was time we got our heads together and talked about this," he began. "And since we both have to eat and I don't often get the pleasure of a beautiful young lady's company, I wondered if you would have dinner with me this evening."

A date? A meeting? Which one was he suggesting? But she didn't take long to answer.

"That sounds fine to me. Shall I meet you somewhere?"

"How about I come around and pick you up, say about six?"

"I'll be ready," she answered, once again hanging up the receiver with a puzzled look on her face.

Eve could not help but hear the conversation and wondered how Willow was going to balance all of this.

The third phone call was to Bobby Carson.

"Hey, there," he was upbeat. "I was wondering if we could go to dinner tonight. I've been thinking about it all day and I'm starved. Say about six?"

"Sorry, Bobby," she was sincere, "but I have plans for this evening. Maybe some other time?"

"Oh, sure," he was dejected. "I know it was last minute and all."

Now she felt absolutely rotten. She hoped she had convinced him that it was something she would like to do.

The evening continued to worsen. When Tim picked her up, his eyes noticed every detail…the white dress with the pink and red roses on it, cut so it showed her shoulders, cinched at the waist with a tiny belt, enhanced by the little white earrings she wore and the sling pumps on her feet. She in turn didn't overlook his trim navy slacks and white button down short sleeved shirt. They made a nice looking couple as they entered *The Place,* a local restaurant. The atmosphere was elegant and Tim O'Toole was a great conversationalist.

"So I understand you're home from college for the summer," he began.

"Yes, taking a slight rest before my senior year," she said "…and of course, to finally find out about my Dad, if I can."

"We'll talk about that soon. I'd just like to get to know you. You lived here all your life?"

"Yes. Grew up here. Family has been here for a few generations…well, at least Mom's side of the family."

"What are you studying in college?"

"I'm going to be an elementary teacher. Not sure where I'll find a teaching job yet."

She was going to include that where she would be teaching would depend on where Scott would be employed.

He studied her face and then smiled at her.

"And you?"

"Easy. Three generations of cops. No choice, I guess," he laughed.

"Because you're expected to be a cop or because you really want to be a cop?"

"No, I really want to be a cop. And I think I'm pretty good at it."

She was quiet and then the waitress was there to take their order. Willow was impatient. She wanted to get to the task at hand, but Tim wanted to have a leisurely meal. When dessert dishes were cleared, only then did he pull out his notebook. He had indeed examined the contents of the file on the accident. Everything that she had found out matched with what he had found. They both agreed that Stace Grant should be the next step and he was okay with her making the contact while he tried to get an interview with the policeman of record.

Bobby Carson left the garage later than usual. No need to get home early since Willow had other plans for the evening. He was disappointed in that. Well, he tried anyway. Just as well. Driving by *The Place,* he noticed a green Chevy…the same green Chevy that Tim O'Toole drove.

Sounds of an impact wrench working on bolts overcame Jeb's country music station on the radio. Bobby knew hard work was a good way of counteracting all the emotions going through his mind. There was a lot of work that had to get out today. And it was unusually hot for June and the garage was already uncomfortable. Bobby looked up from his work when he saw a vehicle pull up to the garage doors.

Tim O'Toole got out of the police car and came into the garage, taking time to get a Pepsi out of the pop machine.

"Sure is a hot one today, isn't it?" he said as he crossed the garage floor to talk with Bobby.

"Yep," Bobby said, grabbing another hand tool from his metal tool box. "But you look like you're keepin' cool."

"That's just the problem," Tim said as he directed his hand towards his Chevy. "No air conditioning. You think you'd have time to look at it? I can leave it. I can use a squad car today. I'm going to go over to see if I can talk to Ken Wells. He was the officer who did the accident report your friend is looking into."

Bobby looked up with a bit of interest.

"How's that going?" he inquired.

"Great. Willow and I had dinner last night. She's a beautiful, intelligent girl."

Emotion crept up inside Bobby, one he hadn't had much experience with, at the bit of information he hadn't been prepared to hear.

"I already know that," he said. "I meant to say how is the case going?"

"Making progress," Tim answered. "Making progress in both areas."

With that remark, he turned and left Bobby with a bunch of questions whirling in his head.

Midmorning he thought about calling her but refrained. Really didn't have a good reason and didn't want to feel rejection again. So it *had* been Tim O'Toole's green Chevy he'd seen outside *The Place* on his way home from work last night. And Willow had been inside having a nice meal with Tim O'Toole. Maybe he had jumped to conclusions thinking they had something going. A figure darkened the door of the garage and Bobby looked up as the shadow passed across the floor. It was Stace Grant.

"Hello, Stace," he said, knowing Stace would hang out most of the day, sometimes talking with Jeb, sometimes just chatting with whoever came by the garage.

" 'low, yerself," Stace replied. "What's up?"

"Not much," Bobby continued to work.

"Gonna be a hot one today."

"Yep. Already is."

Stace nodded in agreement.

Bobby really didn't have time today to just shoot the breeze with anyone who walked into the garage. But then he remembered his promise to Willow about trying to set up something between her and Stace Grant.

"Hey, Stace," he began. "You been around a long time, haven't you? Know a lot about a lot of things."

Stace never was terribly dirty, but he had a way about him that made one think he could spruce up a bit. His hair was long and he had a beard that needed trimmed and there was something shifty about his eyes when he looked you in the face. He always wore jeans and an old t-shirt that advertised some kind of beer or something slightly off color. He was never without a pack of cigarettes, always visible in his chest pocket and his fingers were dirty like he'd been working, something no one ever saw him do. He was married to Julie Jumps and Bobby never heard of any children there. His wife was kind of quiet and he hadn't seen her many times around town.

But Stace could be manipulated and was noticeably flattered at being recognized as a knowledgeable person in the community.

"Where did you work, Stace? I've never heard you talk about anything like that."

"Injured. Never could work. Sad thing. I always wanted to work, just couldn't 'cause of my condition."

Bobby guessed his *condition* might have been laziness, but he pushed on.

"You were in the war, weren't you?"

Stace became slightly agitated.

"Couldn't. Injured. I wanted to go and do my patriotic duty just like all the rest of the fellas and be a big war hero, but they wouldn't take me."

Bobby surmised that being rejected for the service was a touchy point with Stace.

"I've got a friend who is interested in some things that happened back in 1942. I thought you might be able to help her out."

"Well," Stace hesitated.

"I told her that if there was anybody who'd be able to give her information, it'd be Stace Grant."

Stace was caught somewhere between uncomfortable and being impressed with his own importance. Bobby hid the smile that persisted to surface on his own face.

"Well, I suppose I could," he finally agreed.

Bobby thought perhaps he'd said enough for the time being. He had learned to be a pretty good judge of character over the years and it was best to let Stace Grant mull things over and let his ego kick in. Besides, there was a lot of work to get out before the end of the day. He needed to focus.

It was getting somewhere near 6 pm before the work seemed to be coming together. He was bone tired tonight. He'd just said goodbye to his employee, Jeb, had turned the lights off and was ready to leave himself when he saw her standing there. Pink shorts and a white and pink striped shirt and white sandals.

"Oh," he couldn't conceal the jolt the sight of her gave him. "You surprised me. Didn't see you standing there."

Why was his voice so breathless?

"Heard you were working late," she smiled that incredible smile that worked miracles within his chest. "Thought I'd come by to see if you were too tired to go on a picnic up at the state park."

He was thrilled with the idea that she actually wanted to spend time with him.

"I'm pretty dirty," he objected.

"Grab your gear and we'll take a dip in the lake while we're there."

How could he resist such a tempting offer? His thoughts raced ahead of him as he locked the garage doors behind him. She drove and he realized he had never been with her before while she was driving. Although she drove pretty fast, he felt comfortable as he let the breeze from the window blow across his face.

He was a good swimmer, perhaps a stronger swimmer than she was, but she was able to keep up with him and they splashed and dove and dunked each other and all she could remember was his strong arms around her. Wrapped in beach towels, they settled down on a blanket where she spread a picnic meal. Fried chicken, potato salad, rolls and brownies for dessert.

"Did you make all this yourself?" he asked.

"Every bit of it. Slaved away all morning doing it."

"How'd you know I would have said yes to your invitation?"

She giggled.

"Bobby Carson, how long have I known you? Of course you would have said yes."

Picking up another chicken leg, he nodded his head.

A slight breeze had picked up as the evening progressed and moved his hair back and forth. The diminishing sunlight caught his eyes just right and picked up a variety of colors and she remembered that same feeling as when they were kids down by the creek. Yes, Bobby Carson was a good-looking guy. Good build. And his lips were…

"Stace Grant stopped by the garage today."

"Oh," she was brought back from her thoughts to the conversation at hand. "Good. Did you find anything out? Is he willing to talk to me?"

"Well, he indicated he might be willing to talk, if you flatter him enough. But, Willow, there's just something about the man. Can't quite put my finger on it. He got real agitated when I mentioned 1942 and the war. Don't know why. He did say that he was injured and never went to the service. Maybe that was it. Being turned down might have hurt his ego some. At any rate, I'm not sure I'm comfortable with you meeting with him alone."

"Oh, I'm not afraid of him," she protested.

Seeing the concern in his eyes, she added to her protest.

"But if you're concerned about it, I could always take Tim O'Toole with me."

Another emotion played across his face.

"Or I'd be glad to go with you," Bobby added softly.

He stretched out on the blanket after the meal. The sun was setting now and there was a trace of a moon in the eastern sky. It had been a very long day, but he liked the way this one was turning out. He wasn't pleased that Tim O'Toole was in Willow's life, but maybe it was a good thing. After all, she had come to him at the garage, not Tim, with the picnic lunch and they were here together. The last thing he saw before he closed his eyes was Willow's face, her curls moving across her forehead with the breeze and a beautiful smile on her lips. And a tired Bobby Carson slept.

She sat in the sterile environment of the hospital. Scott was so still under the white sheets. Explosion in the chemistry lab. No surprise there. Geeky guys trying experiment after experiment. She chastised herself for that thought. Maybe the term *geeky* was a bit strong; but everyone knew that science students were just a little bit different, living in a world of their own with their formulas and theories.

Sitting alone in the quietness of the room gave her time to evaluate all that had happened to her over the past few weeks…the decision to spend the summer at home, Bobby Carson showing up at the funeral visitation, her progress in solving her father's death, meeting Tim O'Toole, her visit with Hank Robertson. It had been a hectic few weeks. And here she was sitting at the bedside of the man she was about to marry. Funny, that seemed such a long way away. Had she made those decisions in another lifetime? Scott was a great guy. He would be a good provider. She would never want for anything. Well, maybe that part wasn't true. These last few weeks, renewing her friendship with Bobby had been great. Is that what it was? Friendship? Somehow when she was with him, whether it was sitting quietly or splashing in the lake or watching him play ball or doing things on the spur of the moment, he had excited her.

She liked his sense of humor, his intelligence, his spontaneity. Yes, if she was truthful, all of those things were lacking in her relationship with Scott.

But she couldn't leave him now. She couldn't do that to him while he was lying in a hospital bed. But he hadn't called her that often either. Not that she expected him to. If it hadn't been entered into the schedule, it would not happen. Poor Scott. He really did live in a world different from anything she ever wanted.

However, right now, the important thing was to get Scott well. The nurse came in with the news that his latest tests looked good and the doctor would be in shortly to speak with her.

Willow accepted the news quietly. Scott would recover, but his left arm had been injured and would require months of therapy. Scott moved in the bed and opened his eyes. No, now was not the time to tell him she was having second thoughts about their upcoming marriage.

Tim O'Toole was meeting with the officer on patrol the night of Chuck Evans' fatal accident. Officer Wells resided in a rest home now. He was getting feeble and with no family nearby to care for him, he had made the decision to give up his house for the retirement home.

"I've got a cold case," Tim started. "It's a case you worked on, Officer Wells, and I was hoping we could talk a bit about it."

Tim was pleased to see that Officer Wells had good control of his mental faculties and was receptive to being questioned. After Tim presented a couple of the facts surrounding the incident, Officer Wells began to remember.

"Chuck Evans had the prettiest little wife you ever did see," he said with tears in his eyes. "That was the hardest part of my job…having to tell families such tragic news. She sure was a pretty little gal."

Tim O'Toole hadn't met Willow's mother, but if she was anything like Willow, she was indeed pretty.

"Do you recall the sequence of events that night…the night of Chuck Evans' accident?"

"Well, I was patrolling out past the cemetery east of town when I got the call. Someone had reported a car accident on the gravel road out past the Lonely Oak bar. I headed right over there and found the truck off an embankment. Pretty beat up. I was pretty sure no one had survived that, but I radioed for an ambulance and the fire department anyway. There was a guy already on the scene and he was frantic."

"Do you recall his name?"

"No, can't say as I do," Officer Wells said as he rubbed his hand across his chin and shook his head. "Young fella, he was…like the victim. I think they may have been friends the way he was carrying on. He was already down in the ravine and had one of the front doors pulled open."

"So you weren't the first person on the scene," Tim verified.

"No, I guess not…not if you count that feller."

"I run down the side of the ravine to see if I could help, if anyone was still alive. It was easy to see there was no need for the ambulance. The young driver was already dead. And then the other feller, well, he just shoved this piece of paper in my hand. Said he found it next to the driver on the front seat. And that was the suicide note. If it hadn't been for that note, I would have said the young man was just driving too fast and lost control of his vehicle. But there it was…the note, I mean."

"Anything else you recall?"

"Guess that's about it. The firemen came and got the body out of the truck. And when I turned around, the other feller had left and came back with two more young men. When questioned, as I recall, they said they'd all been at the bar drinkin' cause they were going to leave shortly for the service. It's all in my report."

"Thanks," Tim said. "You've been a big help."

"Oh, that's okay. Don't have much to do these days. You know, I never did get used to writing up accident reports where there was a death like that."

He shook his head, remembering the tragedies he had dealt with in his career.

Tim reported to Willow later that evening over coffee.

"His facts seem pretty accurate and consistent with his report I read in the file."

"The other man on the scene was definitely Stace Grant. I need to talk with him next. Bobby seems to think I shouldn't go by myself to see him."

"I could go with you if you want," Tim offered.

Willow thought for a moment.

"We'll see."

"You been out of town? I tried to reach you a couple of times."

"Oh, yeah," she said quietly. "A friend of mine was hurt up at school. But he's okay now."

She wondered later why she just didn't tell him that the friend was the guy she had planned to marry…at least that had been the plan up until this summer.

"You're doing just great, Scott," she encouraged. "Keep it up. Only five more to go."

The physical therapist working with Scott appreciated Willow's presence. He certainly was one difficult patient to motivate. He seemed to try harder when Willow came. And she was there at least once a week for his sessions. Other than regaining the use of his arm, he was progressing rapidly. Psychologically, he lagged behind. At this point, he was quite sure he would never regain the use of his arm.

But Willow had only so much patience.

"Scott, you need to try harder. The doctors say there is no reason for this. Don't you want to get better? Let's get these exercises entered into your schedule. You can do this. If I don't see more progress and more effort on your part, I won't waste my time coming up here."

He scowled at her over his glasses which habitually slid down his nose.

"You wouldn't quit coming, would you?" he pleaded.

"I would if you do not start cooperating. This woman can only do so much. You have to help yourself."

The physical therapist stood nearby and thought perhaps this was what Scott needed to hear as well.

"I'm leaving now, Scott, but I'll be back next week and I'd better hear there has been some effort going on here."

With that, she looked at the therapist who smiled in return and Willow left the rehab facility. On the drive back home, she knew exactly what she needed to do. A little bit of pain now might be better than a whole lot of pain later on.

Taking in a movie with Tim O'Toole seemed harmless enough. It was a funny movie, nothing that would require sentimentality, just something for fun. They stopped afterwards for a milk shake at the local Tastee Freeze and there was some good conversation and some laughs. And she noticed other girls looking at her with envy for being accompanied by such a handsome young man. That made her feel good.

After that, he walked her to the back door of her mother's house and lingered for a time, but he was smooth and it seemed like the natural thing to let him kiss her. And it was nice, but she didn't sleep well afterwards, tossing and turning with many questions in her head.

Chapter Ten

Aroma from the summer roses and spirea bushes wafted across the front porch where Eve and Willow had taken up residence for the evening. It was good just to sit and relax from the busyness of the day.

"It's great having you here, Willow."

"I enjoy being here, Mom. Sometimes when you get away from the things that mean the most to you, you find out what you truly miss in life."

"Oh?" Eve looked up from her embroidery work.

"Yeah." Willow continued. "School is great, but there the focus is on getting through the classes and tests and making the grades and worrying about school stuff."

Eve put the embroidery aside and removed her glasses and massaged her forehead to relieve the tension and waited for Willow to reveal what she really wanted to say.

"I was up to see Scott last week."

"How's he doing?"

Again Eve was being cautious.

"I think he's going to be okay. His physical therapist was pretty frustrated with him so I had to talk pretty sternly to him. I think that probably helped."

"How did you feel about having to do that?" Eve asked.

"Mom, I'm having second thoughts about Scott."

"Umm."

Eve had always let Willow talk through problems with as little interference as possible. She trusted Willow to work through things and make intelligent decisions.

"How did you feel about Dad? I mean, was it head over heels for you?"

"Oh, my!" Eve began. "I think I was in love with your father from the time I laid eyes on him."

"What made him so special?"

"Oh, I don't know. He was funny and creative and I always felt loved and protected when I was with him. He was kind and a hard worker. No one has ever made me feel like he did."

"Did you date other guys a lot?"

"Now we *are* talking ancient history," she laughed. "Not really. Not a lot. I hung out with a group of kids. Went to the senior prom with Greg Hall, but that wasn't anything special. We dated for a while. Dated Stace Grant for a while. That was about the time your Dad and I started dating."

"Isn't Stace Grant one of the guys in the picture with Dad?"

"Yes, but he was very jealous and possessive and I had to tell him that our relationship wasn't going anywhere. He was really angry for a while and I kind of avoided him after that. But your Dad usually included him when he was out with the guys, but he knew how I felt so he was never around me much."

Eve knew Willow was absorbing everything.

"How's your investigation going?"

"Mom, I have this incredible feeling that I am going to uncover something huge."

"You need to be prepared for anything. And then you will have to accept that and let it go," she cautioned.

"That's exactly what Bobby Carson said," Willow added.

Eve pretended not to notice the enthusiasm Willow exhibited when she talked about Bobby.

"You've been seeing a lot of him, haven't you?"

"Yes. We get along really good together and he's lots of fun to be around."

"Umm."

Eve picked up her embroidery and continued to sew.

It seemed like longer than three years since Willow and Alice had shared a banana split, but here they were together once again just like they did in high school, sitting on the high stools at the ice cream parlor; and Willow didn't feel much different than she ever did when she placed the order.

One banana split, extra nuts and two spoons, please.

"So, I take it you're able to eat anything now being past the morning sickness."

Alice laughed.

"It's anything and everything now. Frankie says the grocery bill always goes up about this stage in the pregnancy. Weird cravings."

"You just look terrific when you're pregnant. Well, you always look terrific, but you know what I mean. You have a glow about you."

"Thanks," Alice continued to smile. "I love my life. Changing diapers, cuddling babies, welcoming Frank home at the end of the day, sleeping next to him every night. It's great! It's what I've always wanted. Willow, I am really, really happy."

Willow was happy for her best friend, fighting the wave of sadness that swept over her when she thought about her own life. Yet it seemed as if they had grown apart. That was understandable since they had both chosen different paths in life. For Alice, it had been all about family; for Willow, those family ideas were still just dreams.

"So tell me about this person you plan to marry," Alice prompted.

All of a sudden Willow didn't want to talk about Scott. But she proceeded anyway.

"He's a chemist and he's very smart. Really intelligent. Very structured. He keeps a pretty tight schedule. There will be no problems with him getting a good job and he will get paid a really good salary. He works hard. He leads a very structured life."

"The brainy type, eh?" Alice asked.

"Yeah, I guess so. He works really hard and he's near the top of his graduating class."

Noticing the frown on Alice's face, Willow revamped her description.

"He's tall, not an athlete. He will find a job. Then I will look for a teaching position in that same area. Then we will talk about a wedding.

"In that order?" Alice asked.

Willow laughed uncomfortably.

"Well, I guess you'd have to know Scott. He's pretty focused and scheduled. You'd have to meet him to understand."

Willow suddenly realized she wouldn't even want Alice to meet Scott. Alice would find him boring and uninteresting. Of course, she would never say that, but Willow knew that's what Alice would think.

Alice changed the subject.

"I hear you're inquiring into your Dad's death."

"Yes," Willow was relieved for a change of topic "You know how that's been an issue with me since I was a teenager. I feel like I finally have to set this thing to rest."

Alice was quiet, remembering times when the girls were growing up when Willow had struggled with her father's unexpected death.

"You making any progress?"

"Some. I've got copies of the newspaper accounts, his obituary. I've interviewed one of his buddies he was with the night of the accident. A cop by the name of Tim O'Toole has talked to the officer who was on the scene of the accident. Tim is helping a lot."

"Ooh," Alice reacted. "I've seen him around and he's *really* cute!"

"Yeah, I guess."

Alice raised her eyebrows.

"Okay," Willow admitted. "He is super cute!"

Willow laughed softly and Alice was seemingly satisfied with that response.

"Well, it's nice to know you haven't lost your eyesight."

"I have one more person to interview…another guy who was at the scene of the accident. But Bobby doesn't think I should go alone to do that."

"Speaking of Bobby, have you seen much of him since you've been back?" Alice asked discreetly.

"As a matter of fact," Willow responded, "we *have* done a few things together."

So tell me more about Bobby.

"Oh, just that we've gone out a few times. Well, I guess casually, you might say. He's smart and funny and easy to be with. He's grown up to be quite a good looking guy and I really enjoy his company. He's compassionate and I like that about him. He's spontaneous and I like that about him."

Alice made an obvious assumption. Her best friend's description of the man she intended to marry and the description of Bobby Carson revealed a whole bunch of information about Willow. Alice cleaned out the last little bit of ice cream and syrup from the bottom of the dish.

"Wow, that was really good," she said. "I'm glad we had this time together, Willow. Bring Bobby by sometime and we'll have a cook out or something."

Alice smiled as the two girls walked from the ice cream parlor. Alice knew something about Willow that Willow had yet to learn. All knowledge truly did not come from books.

All the talk with Alice about Bobby Carson made Willow wonder why she hadn't heard from him, so she decided to stop by the garage on the way back from the ice cream parlor. Tim O'Toole's green Chevy was parked outside.

He was the first to notice her when she came through the door.

"She is some kind of girl, isn't she?" he commented to Bobby as they watched Willow who had stopped by the pop machine for a grape soda.

"Yeah, I guess so," Bobby answered, wiping his hands on a shop rag.

"Guess so? Man, are you blind? I've got to find some more ways to be with her. This could be a very interesting summer."

Bobby did not answer and an uncomfortable feeling spread throughout his body.

"Hi, guys," Willow approached. "Anything exciting going on around here?"

"Just got exciting when you came in the door," Tim was quick to pick up on her line.

Bobby just looked at her.

"I just thought I'd come by to check things out and see..."

She stopped, not wanting to reveal her real reason for stopping by.

Tim didn't miss an opportunity.

"I'm glad you're here. I was going to call you again. I really enjoyed our dinner the other week. Think it's about time we did that again."

Bobby tried to catch a glimpse out of the corner of his eye to see what Willow's reaction was, but didn't know if he really wanted to find out.

"Oh, yeah?" Willow said, casually.

"Yeah, how about tonight? I'm free."

Tim was enthusiastic and persistent.

Willow saw Bobby's body tense at Tim's proposition.

"Well, ya know," Willow started. "I really do have other plans for tonight."

"Surely you could break those plans. I promise I will be good company and won't be all talk about the case."

Willow heard Bobby give an audible sigh. She smiled.

"Sorry," she declined, directing her attention towards Tim again.

"You sure? Dinner and dancing? I'm a great guy...good dancer."

"No doubt you are," Willow answered. "How about we talk over breakfast in the morning?"

That seemed to satisfy Tim and he made his way out of the garage much to Bobby's relief. Bobby continued working on the same car he worked on during their conversation. She left his side and walked around the garage looking at things. Bobby stopped to watch her; but when he thought she might be looking at him, he quickly dropped his eyes and continued working on the car. Finally she approached him.

"You going to continue to ignore me?" she asked.

He didn't look up from his work.

"Ain't ignoring you. What gives you that idea?"

"You didn't even welcome me when I came in the garage."

"Didn't have a chance to."

Again he refused to look at her.

"What do you mean by that?"

"Looked like you were pretty busy with Mr. Super Cop."

"Funny."

He continued to work and she continued to stand nearby. An extremely tight bolt was giving him trouble and his hand slipped and he skinned his knuckle.

"Darn it!" he exclaimed as he drew back his hand.

"Here, let me see," she offered.

She moved forward and took his hand in hers to examine the damage.

Looking up into his face, she pronounced, "I think you'll live. Where do you keep the band aids?"

He gestured towards a first aid kit on the shelf and she immediately found what she needed to patch him up.

"Hold still," she admonished.

"Are you sure you've ever done this kind of procedure before, doctor?" he kidded.

"Nope," she responded. "You're my first guinea pig…er, patient."

She didn't know why she was so nervous. Putting a band aid on someone's finger wasn't that big of a deal. But he was standing so close. Her pulse quickened.

Hadn't he had help with band-aids before? But he was so nervous. She was standing so close and there was that familiar scent of her perfume that made him weak in the knees.

"Willow," he whispered her name.

"Yes?" she said, turning her face up to look into his eyes.

"Hey, boss," Jeb interrupted. "you want I should start work on that Buick?"

Willow took a couple of steps back and Bobby cleared his throat before he responded to Jeb's question. Later, when he turned around to look for her, he found her sitting at his desk in his so called office. He walked to the open office door and leaned against the frame.

"You taking over as boss?" he teased.

"Nope," she looked at him with a serious face. "Just thought I might take the boss out to dinner tonight."

"Thought you had plans."

She got up from the chair.

"Oh, but I do have plans," she tormented. "I'll pick you up at 7."

With that, she left and he stood looking after her, wondering whatever was going on in her head. He already knew what was going on in his.

She arrived at 6:45 and he was glad. The panic he'd felt the last half hour or so at the prospect she might not show up was unbelievable. But she did. She wore a mint green sundress trimmed in white with tiny straps at her shoulders and sandals with a cork wedge. Tiny white earrings adorned her ears and a bracelet made of white beads surrounded one wrist. A small white bow was clipped in her curls and one look at her took his breath away.

Her first glimpse of him caused her to have second thoughts. Perhaps she was being too forward. The mere sight of him was provoking strange emotions inside her body. He looked very trim in his gray slacks with a gray and burgundy print button shirt that hugged his waist and flared over his chest and shoulders. But the smile he gave her as he met her at the door superseded everything else.

"Hey," he said. "You're early."

"Too early?" she teased. "Want me to go and come back?"

"Not hardly," he responded, taking her by the arm. "I've looked forward to this all day…well, at least since you left the garage."

They both laughed at that remark and started for the car.

Atmosphere in the out of the way restaurant was casual. Familiar 50's rock and roll music played in the background. He watched her as she ordered ribs and fries and a cherry coke so he ordered the same. Conversation kept them both on their toes with cleverness and joking interspersed with more serious moments.

"Want to dance?" she proposed.

"I would, but I can't," he said in the most serious of voices.

"Why not?" her eyes grew big with disappointment, wondering why he would refuse to dance. She remembered he and his girlfriend had gone to the prom with them.

"You really want to know the truth?" he continued.

"Of course," she was still confused.

"Because I don't dance with girls who have barbeque sauce on their faces," he laughed.

Embarrassed, she quickly reached for the napkin.

"Where?"

He reached across the table to touch her face.

"Right there by your lips," he said as his eyes met hers.

It was a quiet moment, broken only when he spoke. Holding out his hand to her, he watched her as she gracefully slid from the seat and into his arms in one fluid move.

"Come on, Willow, let's dance."

He'd never experienced these feelings before. He'd known Willow all of his life, ever since they were little kids in elementary school. They'd been good friends for years and yet what he felt now was something he'd never known. Her arms stole up around his neck and she buried her face in his shoulder. He inhaled the shampoo from her hair and loved the way it made him feel to put his arms around her back. There was no hesitation, no awkwardness in the dance…just two people holding each other, swaying to the music, each lost in their own set of thoughts.

The music ended and still he stood with his arms around her.

"You ready to leave?" he whispered.

"I think so," she responded.

She let him drive this time and she sat next to him while he drove. He slipped one arm around her as the car inched slowly towards the edge of town. Steering the car over the gravel road, he came to a stop overlooking the lake, the same lake they had been swimming in a few days earlier. He reached across the steering wheel with his left hand to turn off the ignition, being unwilling to remove his right arm from around Willow's shoulder. He relaxed in the driver's seat while she nestled her head against his shoulder.

"How much longer before you go back to school?" he asked.

"Almost two months. Sometimes the whole thing seems unreal."

"Unreal? How so?"

"My life is so complicated. I feel like I've been in a whirlwind since high school graduation. Going off to college, meeting new friends, leaving the security of home, the investigation with my Dad, Grandma's death. Just a month or so ago my whole life was planned out; and now I'm not sure what I want to do or where I want to be. Is that weird?"

She wanted to include more but hesitated.

"That's what life's all about, I guess," he said. "I just find it hard to believe no college guy has swept you off your feet by now."

Was now the time to tell him about Scott? She didn't want to face that. Instead, she clasped his hand that was on her shoulder.

"Oh, I fight them off every day," she laughed.

"I'm glad you have," he said with seriousness in his voice.

He squeezed her arm and she settled in against his shoulder.

"One thing I am sure of," she said.

"What's that?"

"I'm glad I made the decision to be home this summer."

She met Tim for breakfast the following morning. He was dressed in khaki shorts and a polo shirt. *Good,* she thought, *I'm not overdressed.* He *did* have a disarming smile. Alice was right. Tim O'Toole was a good looking guy.

"Been waiting long?" she asked as she slid into the booth.

"Worth the wait," he would not miss the opportunity to impress her.

She ignored the comment and spread the contents of her file folder out on the table in front of her.

"Aren't we gonna order first?"

"Oh, sure," she quickly stacked the papers. "I'll just have coffee and a sweet roll."

Tim summoned the waitress and placed their orders. Then he turned his attention back to Willow.

"You got something going with Bobby Carson?" he asked bluntly.

She immediately blushed. It was time for her to turn off whatever Tim O'Toole might be thinking.

"I have a boyfriend," she blundered ahead and not looking directly at him. Tim O'Toole needed to be put off. He needed to know she was not interested. "He's still at college."

"Really?" Tim sat back in his seat and studied her face for a while. "I kind got the impression that you were available."

"Sorry if I misled you."

"How serious is it…with this guy at college?"

Didn't he believe her? She felt awkward at her reaction to the question, but quickly recovered.

"Serious enough," she lied.

"Like marriage serious?"

"Oh, yes…but not 'til after graduation."

"That's another year, right? A lot can happen in a year," he said. "You might just meet someone who could change your mind."

Breakfast was quiet from there on and the focus was on the investigation. Tim was interested in everything she had uncovered and was pleased at her organization, including her written notes of her interview with Hank Robertson. It appeared the only thing they had left to do was to meet with Stace Grant.

Since she had been a little girl, she had enjoyed shopping with Aunt Flo. Aunt Flo had a flare for style and always offered good advice. It brought back memories of Willow's high school days when every September Aunt Flo helped out with Willow's wardrobe and taught her some things about what to wear and what colors were best for her and some makeup tips. This excursion would be no different. It was a morning of going in and out department stores and dress shops and changing rooms and making fun decisions.

"Willow Evans, is that you?"

Willow turned to look into the beautiful face of Beth Carson.

"Oh, it's so good to see you," Willow said, embracing the young girl. "You are growing up to be one great lookin' girl."

"Thanks," Beth smiled. "I see you're doing some shopping."

"Oh, this is my Aunt Flo," Willow introduced. "We do this shopping thing every year."

"I just have to show you what I've purchased," Beth exclaimed. "I still remember the tips you gave me when you took me shopping years ago."

"Yeah, I remember that, too. That was fun!"

"It's something I'll always remember. Without a mother, I needed a woman's point of view. Bobby did a good job in selecting you to help me."

"He probably didn't have a lot of choices at that time and just took his chances with me."

They both laughed and examined Beth's purchases and Willow and Flo approved adding a couple of minor suggestions such as adding a scarf or a pin as accessories.

After saying goodbye to Beth and when the back seat of Aunt Flo's car had been filled with packages, they concluded their trip with lunch at a fashionable restaurant.

As dishes clanked and waitresses moved about the linen-covered tables, niece and aunt chatted about their purchases.

"That sundress you bought, Willow, is simply beautiful," Flo said. "You'll be a knockout in that. And such a good price!"

"I love it," Willow replied. "I love all the things we got."

Flo looked at her beautiful niece across the table.

"Just think, this time next year we may be looking at wedding gowns."

"Yeah, maybe," Willow took this opportunity to take a long drink from the stemmed water glass and avoid any eye contact.

"Well, that doesn't sound very exciting," Flo continued.

"Guess I have some big decisions to make," Willow continued.

"Does this have anything to do with your investigation into Chuck's death?"

"No, not at all…well, other than the fact that it was the reason I decided to come home this summer. Things have changed since I've been here."

"Oh?"

"Yes, Aunt Flo, I don't think I want to marry Scott anymore."

There. It was out. She had finally verbalized what she had been feeling now for weeks.

"Is there someone else?"

"Maybe. I'm not sure, but I *am* sure that Scott is not the right one for me."

"Then, Willow, you need to tell him," Flo advised.

Willow shook her head in agreement. She had known for a long time that was what she needed to do. She didn't look forward to that confrontation and did not want to hurt Scott. She still thought Scott was a good person, just not at all what she wanted to spend the rest of her life with.

"And," Flo continued "…if there *is* someone else, he needs to know it, too."

It had been a good morning with Aunt Flo.

Tim O'Toole couldn't wait to get to the garage on Monday morning to find Bobby Carson. He always thought he was pretty good at reading people; and found that very helpful in his line of work. If he had to bet on it, he would have wagered there was something going on between Willow Evans and Bobby Carson. Well, now he would ask a couple of questions.

"Hey, Bobby."

"Hey, Tim. How's it goin'?"

"Not too bad. You?"

"Good. Good. The police department need some mechanic work done?"

"No, no. Just dropped by to visit a bit."

Bobby looked up from his work and studied Tim's face. Tim definitely had something on his mind. Sooner or later that would be revealed. Until then, Bobby would just keep on working on the car in front of him.

"Willow…Willow Evans. You've known her for a long time, right?"

"Yeah," Bobby didn't look up from his work.

"You think she's truthful?"

Bobby continued working on the car, moving over to the side and adjusted the trouble light so he could get a better look at his work.

"I'd say so," he mumbled, wondering all the time what this was all about.

"You got a reason for askin'?" he asked after a few minutes had gone by.

"Just something she said Saturday at breakfast."

"Oh, yeah, how'd that go? Any new leads on the case?"

"Not really. Looks like we're down to one last person to interview and so far I can't see anything to dispute what happened."

"Too bad," Bobby responded, "I think she was looking forward to finding something to change that."

"Maybe she should just go back to college and marry the guy she's promised to and let this go."

The words hit hard and Bobby looked up from his work on the car.

"You didn't know?"

He paused.

"You didn't know!"

"None of my business," he said trying not to let his voice shake.

"Well, I need to get to work," Tim said.

His work here was done.

It hit him like a punch in the stomach. And the feeling stayed with him all afternoon. He thought about calling Butch and telling him he couldn't pitch in tonight's game. But he didn't. And he showed up and he pitched. Butch took him out in the fifth inning.

"What's the matter with you?" he barked.

Bobby didn't answer, but threw his glove down and headed for the dugout. He sat there not really paying much attention to the rest of the game. And she was sitting up there in the stands! What on earth did she think she was doing? It occurred to him that perhaps Tim hadn't told him the truth. But that probably was not the case. She had just played him for a fool these past weeks. But it hadn't seemed that way. He was pretty sure she was feeling things similar to what he was feeling.

Finally the game was over and he headed for the truck. He wouldn't even bother to change clothes. Weariness overtook him and it made sense just to go home and get something to eat and go to bed.

But there she was at the truck. Now what was he going to do?

"Hey, there!" she said as he approached.

He grunted.

"You okay?" she asked.

"You saw the game," he muttered. "How'd you think I'd be?"

"Ouch! Not a good day in Muddville!"

"Yeah, I guess."

She didn't know what the problem was, but whatever it was had made Bobby cranky and disappointed her. She made one last effort.

"Wanna go get something to eat?" she offered.

He didn't look at her.

"Not tonight."

She was hurt, disappointed and shocked at his behavior. Her first thoughts were that she had done something wrong. The next emotion was one of tears, so she hurriedly made an exit.

"Some other time then," she said and walked away.

He took time to look after her, wishing he hadn't felt the way he did. Throwing the glove over into the back, he started the truck and threw gravel as he spun out of the parking lot.

"You're home early tonight," Eve said, noticing the look on Willow's face.

"Yeah, sometimes I just don't understand men!"

"Really?" Eve was cautious. "Want to talk about it?"

"It's Bobby," she spouted off. "We have always enjoyed each other's company. I thought he liked me and tonight he just blows me off. I went to the ball field and he just turned me down flat to go get something to eat."

"Maybe he had a good reason...tired or upset about something or not hungry or something else."

"It was his manner, not just that he didn't want to go get something to eat…just like I had offended him in some way. Besides, he's always hungry. No, I've been over it in my mind and I can't figure out why all of a sudden he doesn't even want to look at me."

"Everything okay the last time you two were together?"

Willow thought for a few minutes.

"I've been over it a lot on the drive home. Everything was perfect. Whatever could have happened to change that?"

Alice didn't visit the garage often. As a matter of fact, Bobby couldn't remember her ever being there, but indeed there she was…pregnant and all.

"Hi, Bobby," she said, looking around at the surroundings that were foreign to her.

"Hi, Alice," he responded. "What brings down you here?"

"Lookin' for a job. Do you hire pregnant women?" she teased.

"I have nothing against pregnant women," he countered, "but this can be pretty hard and dirty work."

"You think being a mother and pregnant is a piece of cake?" she chastised.

"Well, no," he stammered.

She laughed.

"I find that I have plenty to do every day, so I'm not looking for a job. I just came by to ask you over for a cookout Friday night. We're having a few people over and thought you might like to come."

His first response was not to accept the invitation. Maybe he should save Friday for Willow just in case she wanted to do something. *How ridiculous that was!*

"Sure, count me in. Should I bring something?"

"No, we're good unless you want to bring something to drink."

"Okay. See you Friday night."

Alice turned and waddled out the door.

Friday night turned out to be gorgeous. The humidity which had dominated the past few days dropped to a comfortable level and a cool breeze from the south made for a beautiful evening. When he saw her car parked out front, he almost didn't go inside. No. Intimidation was not his style. He grabbed the six pack of soda and headed for the back yard. She was the first thing he saw. White shorts and a frilly pink top and barefoot. He tried not to notice and was saved only by Frank pushing their two year old into his arms.

She thought she heard his truck come up the street and had turned to ask Alice who else was invited to this cook out, but Alice had disappeared, chasing after the little one who was just trying out his new found walking abilities. And then there he was…complete with tan shorts and a blue and tan striped pullover shirt. How had he managed to get that tan? And he wore sandals. She'd never seen him in sandals before.

Alice needed help in the kitchen so Willow merely nodded to Bobby and followed Alice who carried the smaller child over her protruding belly. Once inside the kitchen, Willow had to ask the question.

"Why is Bobby here? You didn't tell me he was coming!"

Alice turned from the refrigerator where she was removing an oversized bowl of potato salad.

"I thought you two were having a pretty good summer," she said.

"Here, let me take that," Willow offered as she removed the bowl from Alice's hands.

"It's not that we haven't had our share of fun this summer," Willow whispered, "but he's been acting strange all week."

"Strange how?"

"Well, he's kinda been avoiding me," Willow continued to whisper. "And I can't think of anything I've done to offend him."

Number two child was screaming now and Alice excused herself to change a diaper.

"Go ahead and take the hamburgers out for Frank to grill," she said as she disappeared into the bedroom with the disgruntled child.

Hamburgers in one hand and potato salad in the other, Willow headed for the grill. Number one child had now been put down on the grass and Bobby's hands were free.

"Can you take one of these?" Willow asked him.

"Sure," he answered and relieved her of the platter of hamburgers.

It was a strange evening. Frank and Alice were so consumed with their family that Bobby ended up grilling the hamburgers while Willow set the table and carried utensils and condiments and ice from the kitchen to the back yard. It surely took a lot of patience to raise a family.

"Burgers are ready," Bobby called out and everyone assembled at the table.

Bobby sat next to Willow on one side opposite Alice and Frank on the other. They were able to eat their meal, but it seemed as if Frank and Alice were constantly being interrupted by the children. Finishing her last bite of hamburger, Willow offered to take the older of the two children so Alice could finish eating.

After the conversation dwindled, Bobby made his move to leave.

"Thanks for having me, guys, but I need to get going," he said.

Alice gave Willow a desperate look.

"You needed to go as well, Willow, right?" she pushed.

"Oh, yeah, sure," a stunned Willow agreed.

So thanks to Alice, Bobby and Willow walked towards their vehicles at the same time. Again Willow felt as if Bobby was avoiding her.

"Frank and Alice sure have their hands full, don't they?" she started.

"Yeah."

"But I would say they are very happy, wouldn't you?"

"I guess. We all knew back in grade school that those two would end up together," he said.

"Back then, who did you think you would end up with?" she asked.

"Probably didn't think much about it then. Things change. Sometimes you think your life is heading in one direction, and then it takes a sharp turn."

"I know about that," she responded, suddenly thinking of Scott.

"What do you think makes them successful…Alice and Frank, I mean?"

"Probably because they are open and honest with each other," he said and she saw his face change to something she had never seen before.

"I gotta take off," he seemed in a hurry now. "Bye."

She watched him get into his pickup and saw him lift his hand to wave as she watched the truck until it was out of sight.

"Well?"

It was Alice.

"Oh, you startled me," Willow said as she turned. "Well…what?"

"Did he kiss you?"

"Of course not," Willow pretended the thought had never crossed her mind.

"He should have," Alice persisted. "I saw the way he looked at you all evening. Of course, he made sure you weren't looking in his direction. And you? You're like a cat walking a picket fence. Why don't you just admit that there's something going on between you two and be done with it?"

"I would if I knew for sure what was happening."

"Does he know you have plans to marry someone else? 'Cause I don't know, but you and I have been friends a long time, Willow, and there is a chemistry here that I recognize. I think it's time you made a decision."

"You think?"

"I do. I know about these things, ya know?"

Willow smiled and gave Alice a hug.

"Thanks for the supper," she smiled over her shoulder as she left. "And thanks for the advice."

"You just pay attention to my advice," she called after Willow. "*The only way to see a rainbow is to look through the rain.*"

"I know, I know," Willow replied. "Grandma Bessie's advice."

Alice just chuckled.

Driving west on her way to campus gave Willow time to think things over. If there was one thing her relationship with Bobby Carson had taught her this summer, it was that Scott was not the right choice for her when it came to marriage. He was a nice enough guy and that would make this all the more difficult, but this was her life they were talking about here. Scott *was* boring, just like Alice had said when Willow first told Alice about him at the funeral home. And Bobby had reinforced that fact. But it wasn't just the fact that Scott was boring; it was about Scott and Willow not being a good fit in many ways. Compatibility. Even if things didn't work out with Bobby, she needed to clear herself of the Scott problem. Scott was definitely not the right person to share the rest of her life.

Easy? No, it would not be easy and Scott would come up with the logical reasons why they should stay together. No doubt in her mind there. If she were lucky, he might be involved in some scientific experiment and might not even care that she was breaking up with him. There, she had finally put that into words. Willow was breaking up with Scott.

Eve sat at the supper table alone. Her thoughts had been with Willow and the trip back to campus and Scott. The entire thing had been discussed into the wee hours of the morning and Willow had made a decision. Although Eve thought Willow was making the right decision, she still had her concerns. She played with the food on her plate, moving it around, but she was not very hungry.

"Hey, Babe, I'm starved! What's for supper?"

He came into the kitchen with his hair curled up in a crumpled mess, wiping perspiration from his face.

"There's a roast in the oven with potatoes and carrots," she told him.

She was standing at the kitchen sink, drying a pan when he came up behind her and put his arms around her.

"Um, I love coming home to you," he murmured, placing a kiss on her ivory neck.

She giggled and put her head back against his shoulder.

"Are you sure it's me or the pot roast you're interested in?" she teased.

He whirled her around and found her lips. She, in turn, put her arms around his neck and responded. Running her hand through his curly hair, she kissed him over and over again.

"You still think it's the pot roast, honey?" he whispered.

She nibbled on his ear.

"Not anymore," she whispered. "It's probably the chocolate cake I made for dessert."

She giggled and he laughed.

"That's what I like about you, Evie Joanne, you are the total package…the brains, the looks, the sexiest and a great sense of humor."

"I love you," she whispered.

"I love you, Babe!"

She was not ready to give up.

"My goodness!" she exclaimed. "You get all that and what did I get?"

He knew she was teasing him and he loved it. He loved his Evie Joanne. He grabbed her in his arms and kissed her again and again."

"Pot roast can wait a bit," he said as he held her close.

Scott sat on the bench in front of the chemistry lab where Willow had found him. His head was buried in his hands. Willow sat beside him, wishing there were some easier way to have said what she felt.

"It sounds like you've made up your mind," he finally said.

"Yes," she said quietly.

Silence.

"It's really for the best, Scott," she attempted to ease his pain. "Neither one of us would have been happy. I wouldn't want to do that to you…to us. Look at it logically."

His response was slow in coming.

"You are correct. We approach life from two different viewpoints. I could try to change."

"No," she interrupted, putting her hand on his arm, "I would not want you to change. You are who you are and I am who I am. That's not a bad thing. We are just better people apart than we are together."

"I guess you're right," he conceded. "Oh, my, look at the time! I am late for a lecture!"

He turned to stand, gathering the load of books into his arm. Pushing his glasses up on the bridge of his nose, he briefly turned to Willow.

"Yes, it's for the best," he said with finality. Then he awkwardly shook her hand.

Willow stayed on the park bench for several minutes. She was relieved…relieved the confrontation was over, relieved Scott was not bitter and feeling she had done the right thing. Her shoulders seemed to straighten as the burden lifted.

Now, on to the next issue.

Chapter Eleven

He was miserable, not at all like his usually jovial self. At home, it was Dad and his brother and sister who noticed the bad attitude. At work, Jeb received the brunt of Bobby's foul mood. It had been a full week since they had spoken. He'd heard she was out of town, gone back to campus, probably to see the guy she was going to marry. And the Fourth of July was coming up in a few days and he had such plans, such dreams for that day. Well, at least he had up until a week or so ago when Tim O'Toole had dropped the information on him.

Bobby sat in his work office at the garage, not really wanting to work and certainly not wanting to answer the phone that continued to ring. But work had to go forward so he grabbed the phone with one hand and a pencil with the other. Instead of a customer, it was Tim O'Toole.

"Hey, Bobby, sorry to bother you at work. I've been trying to get in touch with Willow Evans and she just isn't returning my calls. Do you know anything? Have you heard anything from her?"

Did he have to admit that he hadn't? Well, Tim O'Toole's problems didn't need to be his.

"Haven't talked to her. I don't know where she is," he replied.

Sensing certain coldness in Bobby's voice, Tim thought it best to discontinue the conversation.

"Okay, then, if you see her, give me a call or tell her I'm looking for her."

"Is it about the case?"

"Yeah…sure."

Hanging up the phone, Bobby sat with his hands pressed together, wondering where in the world Willow could be and did she ever think of him at all? Well, he had things to do. Besides, he needed to concentrate on his pitching if he was going to be successful in the game tonight.

Zach and Sally were coming for supper. Willow flitted around the kitchen, making last minute adjustments to the table and helping Eve with the food. Sally was a sweet lady and Willow liked her a lot. She'd been good for Uncle Zach and his outbursts were less frequent now as long as he was not around anything that triggered them like fireworks or a car back firing or sudden noises. Through experience, they had established certain things that were likely to set him off so they had developed a list of things to be avoided.

"Hi, little girl," Zach said as he embraced his niece. "You getting' married yet?"

It was something he always said when he greeted her these days. He meant it as a joke.

"No, as a matter of fact," Willow answered with a solemnness that caused him to pause.

"What's that supposed to mean?" he looked serious.

"I just broke up with Scott," she said, surprised at how liberating it was to say that.

"And what did the poor devil do to cause that?"

"Just wasn't the right guy," Willow answered.

"Better to find out now than later," Sally interrupted.

Willow turned to her and smiled.

"What kind of guy was this…this Scott?" Zach continued to press for information.

"He was a chemistry student. He *is* a chemistry student."

"Well, that settles it all right there. Kind of a nerd, eh?"

Willow didn't answer him and continued putting the mashed potatoes into a bowl. She shoved them into Zach's hands.

"Here, make yourself useful."

"Well, now that seems to be the problem right there. She's just too bossy for her own good. Just chasing all those guys away," he said with a twinkle in his eye.

Times were good when Uncle Zach was good.

Stace Grant stood looking out over his property. His unshaven face reflected about three day's growth. Stroking his chin, he allowed maybe he'd shave later and go on into town for a bit. Nothing much happening around here. Julie was in one of her moods nagging him to clean things up around the place. Things didn't look too bad, he thought. Maybe the beer cans strewn in the yard could be picked up and there was that milk crate over there and the grass could use mowing, but then he'd have to go into town to get gas for the mower and who knows if it would work or not. He ought to get rid of the old bicycle frame, but maybe he could use that sometime for something. And there was the defunct air conditioner laying in the yard…the one that had to be replaced because it no longer worked. Some dog had gotten in the garbage cans and that mess needed cleaned up.

Later on maybe he'd pick up some steaks and pull out the old rusty grill he kept forgetting to put away in the shed. The shed probably needed cleaning out, too; and then he'd be able to put the grill away. Yes, steaks sounded real good. It wasn't like they could afford steak very often like the folks over on the other side of town. He rubbed his hand over his greasy hair to keep it out of his face as he pulled the pack of cigarettes from the pocket of his sleeveless tee shirt with the picture of the buxom woman on the front of it. His hands were dirty from working on the car. Maybe he'd have to take it in and let Bobby take a look at it. After all, he didn't need to flare up his knife injury again. He lit up his cigarette and blew smoke which immediately stung his eyes.

Besides, Stace liked it out here away from everyone. No neighbors for a couple of miles at least in every direction. And if he wanted to practice target shooting with one of the guns from his collection, there wasn't anyone around to hear or complain about it. He could easily have been a war hero, too, with his knowledge and ability to handle guns. But fate had dealt him a bad hand; and in his opinion, he'd done the best he could with it. Yep, Stace Grant was happy with living in the country.

That doctor didn't know much when he told Stace he was released to go to work. After all, that guy hadn't been knifed. He didn't know anything about how Stace felt or what he'd gone through. Why, the emotional strain in itself was overwhelming. No, the doctor didn't understand. Actually, maybe no one truly understood him and the rough life he'd had.

Well, maybe he would get to cleaning things up some day, but there was that old wound of his that he didn't want to flare up. Yep, that wound had ruined his life…held him back from attaining his dreams. Here he was forty four years of age and all he had to show for it was one slightly used trailer that Julie's sister had sold them and a dilapidated shed and a car old enough that parts for it were scarce. Where had his life gone wrong? Life surely had not been fair to Stace Grant.

If Eve Cain hadn't been so uppity all those years ago, he could have made a good life for himself. He was a much better catch for her than Chuck Evans ever was. At least he had been then. But Eve didn't want to have anything to do with him. That day she had refused him had ruined his life. It was shortly after that when Stace had been drinking at the Hour Glass, drowning the picture of Eve telling him she didn't want to see him and this jerk started pushing him around and that's when the knife appeared and Stace got stuck. And Stace Grant wasn't going to let anybody push him around, not only some drunken jackass or some snob like Eve Cain.

But Eve Cain was a pretty girl and just thinking about her caused him to remember all the feelings he had for her, maybe still had if he was honest with himself. But that had happened years ago and he had married Julie Jumps instead. Eve Cain was a real lady. Julie wasn't near as pretty or as smart as Eve Cain, but she had put up with him. Well, except for the nagging him about cleaning things up or fixing things. Well, he'd get to it one of these days.

They'd never had any kids. Maybe that was a blessing. Chuck and Eve had a girl. He had heard she was back in town for the summer. He wondered if she was as pretty as her mother.

He finished his cigarette and crushed the butt under the sole of his tennis shoe. Maybe he'd just go into town and stop by the garage and see if he could find somebody to talk to.

Despite the fact that Eve worked a full time job, a garden spot remained a part of their lives which meant there was still canning and freezing to be done. Picking and cleaning and canning vegetables seemed to be an easier alternative to dealing with other problems Willow was facing. She felt good about her conversation with Scott. As much as she had been concerned about talking with him, he seemed to have adjusted quickly to her decisions. Yes, that part of her life seemed to be working out. She felt like her investigation was moving slowly, and thought she had successfully put Tim O'Toole off with her comments about being in a serious relationship, but right now it was Bobby who occupied her mind.

Eve, after working all day, had come home to all the preparation associated with canning and freezing. But Willow was there to help and that made the difference. Willow had already prepared supper so that was a huge help and she had picked green beans so that much was done. Sitting and snapping beans was a great way to catch up with each other.

"I can't believe the Fourth of July is coming up next week already," Eve sighed. "Where is this summer going?"

"Too fast, that's for sure," Willow answered. "School will be starting before I know it. And I still have some unfinished things to do before I go back."

"But the issue with Scott is resolved, right?"

"Yes, I don't think that's a problem anymore."

"And the mystery surrounding your Dad's death?"

"Still working on it, Mom. I know I've not uncovered everything yet. I just have this feeling down deep inside. I've just been struggling with some other things lately."

"Bobby?" Eve asked.

Willow sighed.

"Yeah, Bobby. We've always been great friends and I don't want to lose that friendship."

"As Grandma Bessie would say, *It's always darkest before the dawn.* Well, we'd better get these beans in the jars, or this evening will never stop," Eve said as she stood to return to the kitchen. She stopped midway and turned.

"By the way," she said, "can I borrow your car tomorrow and you take mine in for an oil change?"

"Sure thing, Mom," Willow answered and then realized that meant seeing Bobby Carson.

Eve was long gone by the time Willow woke and made her way to the kitchen. There on the table were the keys to her mother's car as a reminder of what needed to be done today. She poured a cup of coffee and put a slice of bread in the toaster. As she took a jar of homemade strawberry jam from the refrigerator, her stomach did a little leap thinking about making an appearance at Bobby's garage. She took her time munching the toast and sipping coffee and then made her way to the bathroom where she took a relaxing shower. But warm water gushing over her body did not wash away the feeling she had. She moved the clothes in her closet, searching for something appropriate to wear. She chose khaki shorts and a navy blue tee shirt after leaving several other rejected outfits strewn across her bed.

It was almost ten o'clock before she started the car and drove the familiar streets to Bobby's garage. With a sigh, she pulled the keys from the ignition and made her way through the door.

"Hey, Willow, what's up?" Jeb greeted her.

"My Mom needs an oil change in her car," she said, looking around the room which was apparently empty other than Jeb and Willow.

"Yep, I'll get right on it," Jeb said with enthusiasm.

Willow suddenly felt uncomfortable.

"Bobby gone today?" she questioned.

"He called and said he'd be in later," Jeb informed. "I can tell him you stopped by."

""Oh, that's okay," Willow responded, nervously walking around the garage.

"Okay, give me about an hour and I'll have 'er done."

"Maybe I'll just hang around for a while. You said it won't take too long."

"I'll get right on it."

Willow waited but Jeb finished the car and Bobby still hadn't returned so she drove slowly back home. Whatever the problem was that existed between them, they needed to talk about it. At least, she hoped that would help.

Jeb somehow got the message mixed up. When Bobby returned and he reported the events of the morning, he told Bobby that Willow had been in looking for him and he was to call her.

"I'll call her later," Bobby said.

Right now he needed to find a peaceful place where he could be alone with his thoughts.

Willow needed to sort things out. She needed just some quiet place where she could think about her relationship with Bobby and try to figure out what went wrong and why it bothered her so much. Down by the creek was the only solution she could think of…the place she had gone so often as a child, a comforting place. It had been years since she'd been back there and suddenly that was where she needed to be…in the solitude of the woods with the healing powers of nature all around her.

As she pulled her car to the side of the road, she was pleased to see that all the wooded area had not been destroyed by what people called civilization or modernization. Still clad in the khaki shorts and navy tee and having traded in her sandals for tennis shoes, she started walking through the undergrowth, not noticing the bicycle parked off the road some twenty feet away. She picked her way cautiously through the brambles that seemed to have laid stake to the property, pushing them aside and receiving some scratches on her arms as the briars defended their space.

She could see signs of a clearing up ahead and could hear the bubbling of water as it made its way down steam. Being intent on her destination, she looked neither right nor left and therefore did not see the shadow of a man standing in the shade of the tree line.

He watched her approach and thought about turning to leave before she caught sight of him, but something held him immobile where he stood. The sunlight caught her brown curls and gave them a golden glow. An ache in his chest took up residence.

She was delighted that the stream was still intact. The water was just as clear and swift as it had been several years ago; and she removed her tennis shoes and dipped her feet in the cool water, feeling the current moving gently against them. Finding a rock almost large enough for sitting, she balanced herself until she could sit comfortably and let her feet dangle in the refreshing water. Times she came here as a child played across her mind and the peacefulness of this place seemed to comfort her and ease her concerns.

As she thought about Bobby and the past few weeks, she reached down to splash water on her forearms to relieve the burning of the briar scratches and found it refreshing. She was so absorbed with relaxing that she didn't hear him approach from behind.

"You come her often, ma'am?"

She startled and as she did, she lost her balance on the small rock and slid from her perch right into the stream. The level of the water was not deep, but it was just as wet.

"Ooh!" she screeched as she felt the water penetrate the khaki shorts.

She scrambled to get to her knees and then her feet and stood with her hands on her hips, embarrassed by her predicament as he stood on the bank laughing.

Attempting to walk up the muddy bank, she once again slid into the stream.

"Don't just stand there!" she chastised. "Help me out of here!"

He offered her his hand and pulled her up with more strength than she thought.

"I am soaked!" she complained.

"Yep."

"You think this is funny?" she stormed.

"Nope."

"Then why are you laughing so hard?" she challenged.

"It makes me happy to see you slightly emotional," he replied.

"Good," she was adamant. "At least I'm good for something!"

"I'd say you probably have a purpose in life," he teased. "Everybody usually does. Maybe your talent is just that you can make people laugh."

She scowled at him, shaking her head and attempting to push creek water from her shorts.

"You really shouldn't be wandering around these woods unprotected. Not safe for a young lady such as yourself."

"Oh, yeah? Haven't I told you I have a black belt in karate?"

"Really? No, I never knew that about you."

He paused.

"Maybe there's more things I don't know about you," he said softly.

"Like what?"

He did not answer her question.

"I half way expected you to be here," he said seriously.

"Oh, I wasn't looking for you. That's not why I came here, but I can't say I'm surprised to find you here either. It's where we come…you and I when we need to nourish our spirits."

She raised her eyes to look at his face beaming with sunlight. He still had on his work clothes from the garage. His eyes caught the sunlight just right to change their color and she had a moment of remembering when she first noticed that when they were kids.

"It's a place we both came to as kids to be alone and think when we had problems to resolve."

She still didn't understand; and at the same time was still frustrated with him.

"So," she said, "you got a problem to resolve?"

He took his time before he spoke.

"Yeah. This girl I know and think an awful lot of seems to be keeping secrets from me."

She was quiet.

"What kind of secrets?" she pretended not to know.

"Well, I've heard she is engaged to marry some guy. And that may be okay, but I kinda thought she and I had something going on."

"Hypothetically, would she be in big trouble for that?"

"Relationships are built on honesty and I've never known this girl to be dishonest. That's what's so disturbing about this whole thing. She's really a great girl. I've known her for a very long time. She's intelligent and kind and thoughtful and full of life and beautiful. And she really makes my heart do strange things."

"Would you believe her if she told you she was sorry for not being truthful with you? She wanted to tell you several times, but just couldn't bring herself to do it. Would you believe that when she came here a few short weeks ago, she was going to marry the wrong man? Would you also believe her if she told you that because of you and the emotions you've brought out in her these past weeks, she broke up with the other guy who wasn't right for her in the first place? And she really appreciates you pointing out that very fact just by being you?"

She moved towards him, her heart full, her arms open. He enfolded her in his and held her close to him.

"How can a few short weeks make that much difference?" he whispered.

"You aren't the only one who has strange things going on in their heart," she murmured.

She tipped her face up towards his. He looked into her eyes and felt the softness of her curls in his hands. He kissed her lips gently at first; and as she responded, he kissed her passionately. Afterwards, he continued to hold her.

"So that explains why you've been avoiding me. You thought I was promised to someone else. I ended that relationship over a week ago. But I still don't understand how you knew..."

"When Tim came by after he'd had breakfast with you..." he began.

"So that's it! Right! Tim O'Toole. I gave him that information at the breakfast because he kept hitting on me and I wanted it to stop. And he went running straight to you! Geesh! What a guy!"

"How about me believing him? Now that I think of it, he was pretty proud to give me that bit of information. Can't believe I didn't see through that one."

They sat on the bank of the creek, holding hands and watching nature at work...the birds fluttering from tree to tree and warbling their songs, the squirrels chasing up and down the trees, the summer flowers in bloom with their splashes of vibrant color, the gracefulness of the weeping willow tree. A hummingbird with his iridescent colors flitted amid the bright flowers until he found the one that was just right for him, the sweetest one; and putting his beak into the flower, drank until he had his fill. A few minutes later he returned to the same flower and repeated the process.

"I remember that day when we first both came here as kids," he said. "There was something special about you then, Willow, and that feeling inside me that started then has just continued to grow."

"Yes, and you brought me here that night after that horrible sock hop after the football game. I was such a mess!"

"Yeah, you were. I didn't know what else to do. Wanted to kiss you real bad that night, but thought I might get my face slapped, you were so mad."

"You know what I remember?" she smiled. "I remember that you made me laugh in spite of myself."

She was quiet for a few moments.

"Thank you," she said, once again turning to him for the sweetness she desired.

They stayed the afternoon, sitting in the grass, watching the birds, watching the water push around the rocks to meet on the other side. Just as he had said all those years ago, they were to overcome obstacles just like that water going around a rock or a log, but they would reunite on the other side.

Chapter Twelve

It was difficult for Willow to meet again with Tim O'Toole after learning how he had attempted to jeopardize her relationship with Bobby. But she did. After going over the facts of her father's accident one more time, it was decided.

"Today is the day I meet Stace Grant," she announced.

Tim O'Toole would have gone with her, but his chief had asked him to get the auto report on a car accident and he couldn't put it off any longer.

"Let me know what you find out," he told Willow as she exited his office door.

He stood gazing at her as she walked out dressed in yellow capris and a yellow and blue plaid shirt. She sure was one fine looking girl; and now that he had told Bobby Carson about her being pledged to another guy, maybe he would have a chance with her. But right now was not the time. She was headed out to talk with Stace Grant and he had to get over to Bobby's garage and get the accident report. Willow Evans would then be at the top of his list to impress.

Willow headed out of town with a set of directions which she laid on the seat beside her. The Grant place would be about five miles to the south of the city limits. City streets gave way to less traveled roads and then turned to deserted gravel ones. Her car left a trail of dust behind her.

It was a steamy afternoon, approaching the first of July. Rain had been scarce the past week or so and already crops in the nearby fields looked as if they were thirsty. Weeds growing in the ditches were covered with dust from vehicles traveling up and down the road.

Willow had a sense of excitement mixed with uncertainty as she drove the five miles. Was she really near the end of her quest for the truth? And what if the truth had always been there and it was indeed a suicide? After all, all the evidence pointed in that direction. Again, she went over the story in her mind...her mother's memories of that night, the things Hank Robertson had told her, the newspaper accounts. Still, if there was something yet to be uncovered, she needed to find out. Perhaps Stace Grant was the answer. Perhaps he knew something, one little shred of information that would change the outcome.

She slowed the car as faster speeds were throwing gravel up against the wheels and she didn't need to get the paint chipped. Bobby wouldn't like that. She smiled as she thought of Bobby and having resolved the issues with him. She thrilled to his kisses and felt so secure in his arms, a feeling she never felt with Scott.

Thank God she had come back home for the summer. And how lucky she was that Bobby had shown up at Grandma Cain's viewing at the funeral home. And didn't Alice know all the time? Isn't that what she tried to tell Willow right from the beginning? Even then, Alice had described Scott as boring. Was she trying to tell Willow then she was making a mistake? But things had been corrected. She had broken things off with Scott and finally she and Bobby had figured out what happened. The only thing she hadn't resolved was letting Tim know she knew what he'd done. And now hopefully her quest for information was about to be resolved.

Up ahead, she saw a curl of smoke off to the right. Surely she must be approaching the Grant home.

Stace Grant was up early that morning. Julie was going to her mother's for the day and he was looking forward to spending the day doing as he pleased, like that was any different from any other day in Stace Grant's life. But, after all, he needed his rest. Ever since that knifing incident at the Hour Glass, the one that had kept him from serving his country and the one that kept him from getting a decent job, he'd had to take good care of himself.

Maybe his government check would come in today's mail. That would be a bright spot in an otherwise crappy day.

Clad in only his underwear, he walked from the kitchen where he'd prepared his own breakfast of bacon and eggs to the bedroom where he pulled on the same dirty jeans and shirt he'd worn for the last...well, he couldn't remember how long it had been. Maybe he'd put on a clean pair of sox today even though it wasn't Saturday. Rubbing his fingers through his greasy hair and picking bits of bacon from his yellowed teeth, and taking a rifle from its place on the wall, he opened the door to the trailer and blinked in the bright sunlight.

He set the trash barrel on fire, ignoring the putrid smell that emitted from it. He let the things that fell to the side just stay where they dropped.

The grass had grown up around the lawn mower which was amusing if you stopped and thought about it. Lighting up another cigarette, he threw the empty package to the ground where it probably would remain the rest of its life. He checked the chamber of the gun to make sure ammunition was present. Might as well do a little target practice before it got too warm. Then he'd find a nice cold beer and just relax a bit.

Bobby was up and into the garage early. He needed to catch up on paperwork he'd been putting off before Jeb got into work. Somehow everything in his life had a bit of zest in it today. He anticipated getting through the day's work so he could spend time with Willow. It was such a relief for him to find out how Willow felt about him. The feeling started at his toes and worked its way up throughout his entire body. And the feeling stayed with him no matter what he was doing.

"Hey, boss," Jeb was at the door. "Good to hear you humming again."

Bobby wasn't even aware he'd been doing it. But nothing could bring him down today.

" 'Mornin', Jeb. Let's get started on that red Dodge this morning. And then an oil change for the Simpsons and then we'll tackle the '52 Chevy."

Jeb smiled.

"Good to have you back, boss."

Jeb immediately started working, glad to have Bobby back to his usual self. He liked working for him. Bobby finished the paper work, returned a couple of calls and made notes in the scheduling book. Pushing himself back from his desk, he stood and was just going through the office door when Tim O'Toole entered the garage. Bobby was less than thrilled to see him.

"Mornin', Tim," he mumbled.

"Mornin.' I'm here to pick up your report on the accident from last week."

"Okay. It's ready."

But he couldn't refrain from saying more.

"About Willow…what you said last week," he began.

"Yeah, I just left her a few minutes ago."

Why not add fuel to the fire? He already had planted the seed last week.

"Yeah, she was on her way out to see Stace Grant."

Something clicked in Bobby. Uneasiness settled in the pit of his stomach and the hair stood up on the back of his neck. He went to his office and got the report for Tim. He didn't wait for any more conversation.

"I need to go," he said and was in his pickup truck and down the road heading south before Tim had ever reached the garage door.

He couldn't explain what he felt. He had no concrete basis for what he was feeling, but he just knew he needed to get to Willow as soon as he could. He left the paved road and skidded in the gravel, but he refused to slow down. Something bad was about to happen.

Apprehension filled Willow's body as she gently pulled the car into the two tracks Stace referred to as his driveway. She could smell the stench of burning trash from the barrel as she shut off the engine. Stace Grant was sitting in a lawn chair near the dilapidated trailer, puffing away on what was his fifth cigarette of the day, one hand closed around a can of beer. Deciding against taking any notes with her, she carefully opened the car door and stepped to the ground. She hoped no mongrel dog lurking out of sight would come around the side of the trailer and surprise her. She moved forward and Stace, although he turned his head to watch her, did not offer to stand up from his comfortable position.

It was just at that time that Willow decided to present herself differently to the unkempt Stace.

"Hello," she called out.

"Howdee," came the reply.

She walked closer and now she could see the color of his eyes; and in one quick glance, took in the dirty clothes and unkempt beard and greasy hair...and the gun sprawled across his lap. But she had come on a mission and could not retreat until she had asked the questions she had come to ask.

She felt like the westerns of old, that perhaps she should yell out *I come in peace,* but she continued moving forward, feeling the tall grass tickle her legs.

"You lost?" Stace looked up at her.

"That depends," she said bravely. "Are you Stace Grant?"

"Depends on who wants to know. You government?"

Willow smiled to herself.

"No, I'm a reporter doing a story," she lied. "Someone in town told me you were a good source of information."

What was it Bobby had told her about Stace? He liked to be flattered. Well, that was the plan of attack.

Stace somewhat straightened up in his chair. She had gotten his attention.

"Well, I am sometimes referred to around these parts as a man who knows a thing or two."

"Good," she continued. "First of all, how long have you lived here?"

"Oh, all my life…well, not in this place, but in this area."

"Then I have indeed found the right person."

At that Stace got even more interested in his guest. He straightened up a little taller in his chair.

"You from around here? You sure do look familiar to me," Stace had a few questions of his own.

It was about that time their attention was turned to a second vehicle coming towards them at a tremendous rate of speed through the ruts. Screeching to a halt, Bobby was out of the truck and at her side in a flash.

"Hey, Bobby," Stace said. "This sure seems to be my day for company. What brings you out here?"

Bobby gave a concerned look to Willow and stammered a bit.

"Oh…uh…er…you said you were having some problems with your old car the other day and I just happened to be in the neighborhood so I thought I'd stop by."

Then his eyes fell on the gun.

"You doin' some huntin'?"

"Naw, just a little target practice. Gotta keep sharp."

"This here's a reporter lady come to interview me," he said, gesturing towards Willow. "Sorry, didn't catch your name."

"Hilda," Willow quickly responded, having no idea where that came from. "Hilda Hunt."

Bobby looked at her suspiciously, gave her a nod of acknowledgement and then continued his conversation with Stace.

"You care if I hang out a bit?"

"Nah. Nah, go ahead."

Bobby moved a short distance away…far enough so Stace wouldn't be concerned, but close enough if Willow needed him.

"Now, missy, what is it you want to know?" Stace asked.

"I'm doing a piece on what it was like here during the war, right here in this community. I'll bet you were what about that time? In your early twenties?"

"Yes, ma'am," Stace was excited. "Those were great times."

"You must have been a handsome young man then," she continued. "Well, not that you aren't now, you understand; but I can imagine you in those days."

Bobby, standing far enough behind Stace so he couldn't be seen, rolled his eyes at her and grinned. Willow was laying it on thick.

"Did you serve in the armed forces?" she asked.

"Oh, I wanted to, ma'am," Stace said proudly. "Wanted to serve my country. I'm good with a gun."

With that, he shouldered the rifle and quickly took bead on a rusty tin can on a leaning fence post, pulled off a shot and hit the can square in the middle.

Willow tried to hide the fear that brought to her body and continued the questioning while Bobby stepped forward.

"Mind if I have a look at that?" he asked as he reached to take the gun out of Stace's hands.

"Sure thing," Stace was proud. "She's a good 'en."

Willow drew in a deep breath.

"Now where was I? Oh, yes, you and being in the service."

"Yep, I was all set to go, I was. But got into an unfortunate scrape and got injured. Bothered me ever since."

He rubbed his side as if the memory had brought about some physical pain.

"I imagine you hung around with guys who went in though, didn't you? I have the names of some right here in my purse. Let me see if you remember any of these fellas."

With that she searched through her purse and brought out a small notebook and pencil. Flipping through the pages, she pretended to search for the names.

"Oh, here we are," she said. "Bill Smith."

"Never heard of him," Stace shook his head. "Are you sure he was from around here?"

Ignoring his question and relieved he didn't know someone by that name, she went on with her list.

"How about Jerry Wells?"

"Oh, yeah, I knew Jerry alright. Pity, though. He never made it back. Nice guy."

Willow threw in a couple of other bogus names to keep him thinking. Bobby glanced at her now and then as he pretended to tinker with Stace's vehicle.

"Did you know a Hank Robertson?"

"Yes, indeed. Now Hank was one fine feller. He went across and gave the enemy hell and got hisself back here in one piece. Can't say as I know what happened to him though. I heard tell he married and moved somewhere after he got back. You know, I always was a good shot. If'n I had the chance, I could have been one of them war heroes."

"I imagine you could have," Willow persisted. "Now, how about Chuck Evans? Did you know him?"

At the mention of Chuck's name, Stace sat forward in his chair and his eyes narrowed and he appeared to be agitated. Bobby's full attention was on Stace and Willow.

"Yep, I knew Evans alright," his voice seemed strange. "Nice enough guy, I guess. He and I were never close, you might say. Guess you can say he was on the arrogant side."

Willow was breathless.

"Do you know what happened to him?"

Stace grew uncomfortable and twisted in the old lawn chair. He took time to light up another cigarette and looked at her through squinted eyes.

"I heard tell he was in an accident before he shipped out. Took his own life, he did."

"Do you find that strange, Mr. Grant? Ready to go to the army and then take his own life?"

"Can't say. That's about all I remember."

It was clear that Stace Grant was ready for this interview to be over. Willow was quite sure she had all the information she was going to get from Stace Grant today.

"I need to talk with Bobby now about my car."

"Okay, thank you for talking with me. Could we perhaps talk again another time? You really have been a huge help to my story, but I *do* have more questions."

"Sure. Another time," Stace said as he struggled to get out of the chair.

"Nice to have met you, Miss..." Bobby said with a satisfied smile on his face.

"Miss Hunt...Miss Hilda Hunt," Willow said cordially.

"You sure do look familiar. Are you sure we've never met?" Stace asked, carefully scrutinizing her face.

"Don't think so," Willow replied. "Thanks again for your help. I'll look forward to doing another interview with you real soon."

She was about to leave, but turned for one last comment.

"Let me make sure I have the name right," she smiled. "It's Grant with a G, correct?"

"Oh, yes, Grant," he puffed up. "Stace Grant. S-t-a-c-e."

She smiled as she pretended to write the information.

Willow drove slowly back down the gravel road until she saw the dust from Bobby's pickup in her rear view mirror. She pulled over and he pulled in behind her.

"What did you make of all that?" she questioned.

"He's definitely hiding something," Bobby agreed.

"Yeah, denying he knew my Dad when he's in the photo, he was drinking with the guys that night and he was first on the scene of the crash. Something definitely is not right."

"Can I pick you up tonight about eight, Miss Hunt? Hilda Hunt? How did you ever come up with that name?" Bobby smiled.

"I don't know where the *Hilda* came from," she explained, but the *Hunt* came when I looked at the rifle placed across his lap. That was a might scary, especially when he took that shot. Thank goodness you were there. By the way, how did you know I was there?"

"Tim O'Toole stopped by the garage and told me. I just got a funny feeling about it."

Chapter Thirteen

"I want to see exactly where the accident occurred," Willow said. "Would that be too painful for you, Grandpa?"

"No, I suppose we could do that. I think I can remember the way."

Traveling east out of town in Willow's car, she carefully followed the dirt road otherwise known as Route # 6.

"Now if my memory serves me right," Grandpa Cain mused, "the Hour Glass bar should be coming up soon on our left. It's right after the new nursery place that just opened not long ago."

Sure enough, Willow saw the signs for the nursery and started watching for the Hour Glass. It didn't come as soon as she expected and her anticipation level was increasing. Then came the flickering neon lights which looked totally out of place in broad daylight. The building looked so deserted in the afternoon hours and Willow thought their appeal certainly must be stronger with the coming of nighttime. So this then was one of the last places her father had been before his death. Her chest tightened at the thought.

"Now I figure we need to go about another couple of miles," Grandpa continued to narrate. "There should be a big sycamore tree on the left and then a sharp curve in the road to the right and that's where the car went over."

With those words, he choked a bit as he remembered the horrible night and they continued to ride in silence. Willow thought it was the longest two miles she had experienced. Then quite suddenly the giant sycamore loomed into sight and Willow slowed the car and made the turn to the right.

"Here!" Grandpa raised his voice.

Willow stopped the car and, getting out, proceeded to peer over the side. Indeed the scene was grim as she imagined a vehicle careening over the edge of the slope and falling an estimated twenty feet or so below. Not just any vehicle, but her Dad's vehicle. Not just any driver, but her Dad driving to his death. She shuddered as she looked down, seeing a piece of fender peeking through the weeds, still there as a gruesome reminder, a memorial of sorts.

"I'm going down," she said as she turned to her grandfather.

"You think that's wise?" he was concerned.

"I'll be fine."

With that, she started down the steep slope, slipping and sliding as she went until she reached the flat area that had broken the car's spiral. She didn't know what she was looking for or didn't even know she would recognize something as important if she did find anything. She walked the area for several minutes, stopping at last near the lone piece of fender. As she stood there, she thought she heard a slight whisper... *Willow.*

Now she was dreaming. She looked around half expecting to see someone standing there. Had she actually heard something or someone? Or was it just her imagination playing tricks on her? But the feeling that came over her, a sense or a connection with someone caused the hair on her arms to stand up. She rubbed them in response. Looking around once more, nothing had changed, no sounds came at her from behind trees or bushes so she started the climb uphill towards the car. It had been easier coming down than going up. She had to work really hard and grab onto saplings to aid in her trek. Finally she reached the top and was welcomed in Grandpa's arms as he had become agitated and was standing outside the car.

"You're shaking, Willow," he said as he embraced her.

"It was really weird, Grandpa," she answered him, feeling the comfort of his arms.

"What? Tell me."

"I would have sworn I heard a voice whispering my name when I was standing there," she was almost in tears.

Grandpa Cain hugged her tightly.

"That was your Dad, sweetie. Now I'm convinced he wants you to find the solution to the past."

The next few days were days to recover. She shared the events of her trip with Grandpa Cain to the scene of the accident with Bobby. She did not share them with Tim O'Toole or even her mother. The Fourth of July celebration was coming up so she decided to wait until those festivities were over before she made another overture to Stace Grant.

Fourth of July meant a carnival in town. It meant one of Bobby's baseball games in the early afternoon and lots of neighborhood activities.

"I'll pick you up about 10," Bobby said. "We'll just spend the entire day…if that's okay with you," he added.

"I'd love it."

Watching horse races took up most of the morning hours at the track where they made bets with each other on the winning horses. When the total was complete, he owed her fifty cents. From there they went to the crafts tents and she bought a wooden *Welcome* sign decorated with pink and yellow flowers.

"Now, whatever are you going to do with that?" he asked as he carried it back to the truck.

"Well, maybe someday I will have my own place and I'll put that by the front door to welcome people to my house."

"And where will this house be?" he asked.

She stopped.

"I don't know," she said seriously. "I guess I have to get a teaching job first."

She hadn't given it a lot of thought, but now decisions such as those seemed to be getting closer.

"I sure hope it's not too far from here," he murmured.

Her heart leaped at what that could mean.

By that time, they had reached the truck and he put her treasure in the back. He reached for her hand and squeezed it gently. No, she did not want to be far from here.

They ate corn dogs and drank root beer for lunch. He would be pitching in the early afternoon game so he didn't want to eat much.

It was a scorcher either sitting on the bleachers in the hot sun or pitching nine innings, but it was worth it when the red team beat the visiting team 12-8 with Bobby hitting a fly ball way over the right fielder's reach and circled the bases. He saw her standing up cheering as he rounded third and headed for home and at that point he thought his feet sprouted wings and flew the rest of the way to score the winning run.

She met him outside the dugout and they headed arm in arm towards the truck, midst shouts from supporting fans and fellow players. He was sweating profusely and asked her to drive. She felt privileged since she was pretty sure Bobby didn't let just anyone drive his pickup.

"Let's pick up some swim gear," he suggested, "and head on out to the lake and cool off."

"Good idea," she agreed as she herded the truck through the streets.

It was refreshing...the lake waters now warmed a bit from the summer sun, but cool enough to be enjoyed. Not nearly as cold as it was earlier when they had first taken a swim. At first, it was just refreshing to dip under the water and come up together, laughing and enjoying the freedom. Then they decided to actually do a little swim over to a small island not far from the shore. There they sat in the shade of a small grove of trees as they held hands and talked.

"Willow," he said, thoughtfully, "have you given any thought to where you might like to teach?"

"Not until now," she responded, playing with a lock of his hair. "Why?"

"It's something you really want to do, isn't it?"

"Yes, it's something I've planned for a long time now. And I think I will be good at it."

"No doubt in my mind there," he was confident.

He was quiet for some time.

"You got something on your mind?" she finally asked.

"Yeah."

But there was no further conversation. He turned to her and kissed her and he'd never felt anything like if before. It was a feeling he had waited all his life to experience. Willow was indeed special to him.

She returned his kiss with ardor. She had never experienced these feelings. This surely must be what Alice and Frank had.

After a time, they swam back to shore. He put towels on the seats of the truck and drove her back so she could change into those white shorts and that pink frilly blouse and then to his house where he changed into black shorts and a turquoise plaid shirt. By that time, both were starving so they went to a small café on the other side of town where they ate the blue plate special of the day. Then back to the carnival where loud music and bright lights lit up the midway. He did the gun shoot and won her a teddy bear and they rode a couple of rides before it was dark enough for the fireworks to begin.

"I know the perfect place to watch these," he said, taking her by the hand.

He drove up on the road that overlooked the lake where they had taken their afternoon swim and brought the pickup to a stop. The lake looked so peaceful and calm in the darkness and then the bursts of color began. They sat in lawn chairs in the back of the pickup and watched as brilliant colors of green and blue and reds and oranges spread above them across the sky. She felt the strength in his shoulders as she snuggled against him and he stole a glance at her; and as the lights from the fireworks reflected in her eyes, he knew what his heart had known for a long time.

The sun was already high in the sky by the time she woke, it having been late when Bobby had kissed her good night at the door. She stretched and yawned and then settled deeper into the bedding as she remembered the wonderful day they had. Her heart swelled with pride as she relived Bobby's home run and how much fun the entire day had been and most certainly those time when they'd kissed and felt those tingling sensations. She would have stayed longer in that little world of utopia had not the telephone insisted on ringing.

"Morning, beautiful," his voice was soft and full of emotion.

"Morning, yourself," she whispered. "What are you doing up so early?"

"Early?" he laughed. "The garage has been open for hours."

"What time is it?" she was alarmed, looking around to find a clock. "Oh, my gosh," she said, "is it really 10 o'clock?"

"Yep. Guess I wore you out yesterday."

"Oh, not on your best day!" she took the challenge.

"Good, 'cause you and I have a date tonight."

"Oh, really?" she teased. "What makes you think I don't already have plans?"

"Do you?"

"Just with the guy from the local garage who's taking me…where?"

"Can't tell. It's a secret…a surprise! Wear old clothes though. You'll need them."

"Good," she answered with doubt in her voice. "I like surprises…at least I think I do."

He laughed at that and agreed to pick her up about 7 o'clock. She anticipated all afternoon, racking her brain to try to figure out where he might be taking her.

In the afternoon, she put on a skirt and blouse to make an appearance at the police station. The officer on duty acted a bit surprised when she asked for Tim O'Toole who came from his office all excited that she had made the effort to come down to the station. He greeted her warmly and escorted her into her office.

"What brings you by, Willow?" he began. "Not that you need a reason. I'm always glad to see you."

She smiled but cringed on the inside when she thought of how he had almost ruined her relationship with Bobby by telling him she was engaged. Not that the facts were wrong, but that he used the information to try to come between them.

"I'm here because I would like to see the file on my Dad's accident. You've told me what was in there and I believe you. I...I...well, I'd just like to see for myself. Maybe I can pick up on something we've missed."

She thought the use of the word *we* was a nice touch.

Tim looked around a bit.

"I guess there's no harm in that," he said and promptly went to a file drawer where he removed a manila envelope marked *Chuck Evans,* followed by a case number. He poured the contents of it on the desk in front of her.

"Would you like some privacy?" he asked.

Well, perhaps he did have some sort of manners or compassion or whatever.

"No, that's not necessary," she replied.

Tim continued sorting papers on the other side of the desk, but could not concentrate on his work while his eyes continually wandered over to Willow. Her chestnut curls were intriguing and he wanted to feel them in his hands. And her lips. How great it would be to be able to...

She found nothing out of the ordinary, nothing she didn't already know about other than some snapshots of the crime scene. She shuddered at seeing those. Then she came to the suicide note. Just touching it gave her a feeling of uneasiness. She studied it carefully, trying to find a clue...any clue.

My dearest Eve, forgive me but I can't go on.
Chuck Evans

Trying to think logically while she was overcome with emotion was difficult. The handwriting suggested that it may have been scribbled in a hurry. It certainly was short and to the point. Suddenly she rose from the chair with the note in her hand.

"Is it possible that you can make a copy of this for me?" she asked. "I mean, it wouldn't be illegal or anything, would it?"

"Under the circumstances, I don't think it would be."

He took the note from her and returned a few minutes later and presented her with the copy, putting the original back into the file.

"Thanks," she was in a hurry now. "I've got to go."

He stood there with the file in his hand, looking after her, wondering what she could have found that was of that much interest. Putting the file back in its place, he continued with his paper work, stopping now and then to recall the girl who had moments ago sat across from him at his desk.

Willow hurried into the house. She wanted to do this before Mom got home from work. No need to upset her further with what might be false hope. Where had she put it? It had just been a couple of weeks ago since Eve had shared the poem with Willow…the poem Chuck Evans had written to his wife. Willow searched through drawers and then remembered the small box…the one Willow had refinished for her mother on that long ago Christmas. That surely must be where it was. Her fingers trembled as she opened the box. Sure enough, there it was, the paper yellowed and worn where it had been opened and folded and spotted with tears. Carefully opening it and laying it flat on the table, Willow reached inside her purse and spread out the copy of the suicide note beside it. It was just as she had suspected. The handwriting on the poem and that on the suicide note did not match. At least that was her unprofessional opinion. She sat down at the table with the papers in front of her to absorb what she was feeling. Then hurriedly replacing the poem into the little box, she put the other paper back in her purse.

"How was your day?" Eve asked as she came in the back door.

"Actually, I believe it was a fruitful day, Mom," she replied.

"You going out again?" Eve continued, noticing Willow was putting on a bit of makeup although she was donned in faded jeans shorts and an old shirt. "Where are you going dressed like that?"

"Bobby says it's a surprise," she smiled. "And you know how I like surprises!"

And I know how you like Bobby, Eve thought to herself.

Bobby was secretive about the evening, but she helped him pack the back of the pickup with some bags full of groceries and an assortment of tools. She wanted to ask, but refrained. After all, she was pretty content to sit beside him in the truck as he drove out into the country. Actually, Willow wasn't sure where they were because she didn't think she'd ever been this way before. But apparently Bobby knew where he was going and she trusted him.

She estimated they had been driving about forty five minutes before he turned up a long lane which culminated in front of a log cabin. Still she was confused. An older man in bib overalls and work shirt came out the front door of the cabin and greeted Bobby with a hug and a slap on the back. Then he turned his brown eyes peering out from under bushy eye brows to Willow.

"Oh, Clem, this is Willow. Willow, Clem," he introduced.

Willow could see the sparkle in the old man's eyes. He looked at Willow and looked at Bobby and then spoke.

"Can I hug her, too?" he chuckled.

"I don't know," Bobby grinned. "I guess you'll have to ask her."

Clem looked hopefully at Willow and she opened her arms for a hug. He reminded her somewhat of her Grandpa Cain. And the hug seemed to satisfy him.

Bobby removed the grocery bags from the truck, handing some to Willow and she followed him into the cabin and put them on the kitchen table. Clem was just like a child at Christmastime as he removed the food and put it either in the refrigerator or cupboards, carefully saving out a bag of gum drops. As Willow looked around, she thought the place could use a woman's touch, but it appeared to be fairly clean although sparse of anything extra. She observed a photograph of a man and a woman who she assumed was Clem and his wife at a young age.

"What we fixin' tonight?" Bobby inquired, turning his attention to other things.

"I guess it'd better be the fence," Clem said, "seein' as how the cow got out last night."

"How'd you get her back in?"

"She likes apples and I just put a couple inside the fence and she figured it out."

He chuckled again at his own cleverness. Bobby began taking tools out of the truck and handing them to Willow to carry. Together they headed towards the fence that needed mending and Bobby started working, carefully guiding Willow along in the process. Clem mostly stood beside them and talked as if he was starved for company and Willow was pretty sure he was. It took most of an hour, and although the evening had somewhat cooled, perspiration spread across foreheads.

As Willow looked around, she saw a lot of things that perhaps needed repair, but that would not be for tonight. They sat on the porch a bit...Clem in an old rocker heaped with blankets to soften the seat, Bobby standing against the roof support and Willow sitting on the step. Clem told stories of his ancestors coming to this area and how he'd farmed and married and raised six children right here and got tears in his eyes when he talked of his wife's death and the children that were spread all over the country.

"Anything else I can do for you while I'm here?" Bobby asked.

"I thank ya kindly for your help, Bobby boy, but that's enough for one trip. Next time maybe," he said, struggling to get out of the chair and sensing it was time for his company to leave.

"As the three of them approached the truck, Willow saw Clem grab Bobby by the arm and say, "She's a keeper. Better not let her get away."

Willow smiled as Bobby acknowledged the old man's advice.

The ride back was a quiet one.

"So what's his story?" she finally asked.

"Met him by mistake about four years ago. Someone told me there was an antique auto up here on the hill for sale so I came to investigate. That's when I met Clem."

"Did you find an antique auto?"

"Nope, but I found a man who needed a friend and ever since then I've been comin' up here every week or so to lend him a hand. Well, actually, sometimes I think he makes up things for me to do and I kinda make up excuses to see him. He's a good old guy and lonely, too. None of his children live close by and don't keep in touch that much. I don't think they have a clue that their Dad needs them."

Willow looked at Bobby's face softly lit from the dim lights of the dashboard. This was a wonderfully caring individual and her heart welled up inside her to think he was in her life.

He closed his arm around her and pulled her to him and they continued the drive in silence.

They sat on Eve's front porch swing for a long time. She needed to share with him.

"Bobby, I just *know* the two pieces were not written by the same person," she told him.

He listened intently.

"That's serious, Willow."

"I know. I have a copy of the note from the accident, but I put the poem back in Mom's little wooden box."

She showed him the note.

"It may be difficult since it seems to be scribbled and written in a hurry."

"There's a couple of things that stand out in my mind," she said as they scrutinized the piece of paper under the dim porch lights.

He looked closely at the paper.

"I know that when my Dad was being close with my Mom, he always called her Evie Joanne...by both of her names. And what about *I can't go on?* That doesn't sound right either."

"And how about the signature...*Chuck Evans.* If he was writing to your mother, why would he sign his name like that? Wouldn't it have been *Love, Chuck* or something like that?"

"Yes, that's way too formal," she responded. "And how about the writing?"

"So, if he did write the note, just when did he do that? When would he have had time to write the note? If he had planned it, would it have been scribbled in a hurry?"

"Still a lot of unanswered questions," she said once again folding the piece of paper and tucking it into her purse. "Maybe Tim O'Toole can hook me up with a handwriting expert. He could tell us for sure."

They sat for a long time, the comfort of his arm around her shoulder and holding hands, each with their own set of thoughts.

"I could stay here forever," he said, squeezing her shoulder.

"Me, too," she agreed. "But...you have a job to get to tomorrow."

He left her with the promise of another day...another day together.

Going into the garage to work didn't seem like a chore although he had stayed in bed a little longer this morning dreaming of Willow and how she trusted him with the information she was discovering about her father's accident and how she seemed to be as touched by helping Clem as he was.

But here he was at work and there was a lot of work, so much that he had his brother, Brian, come in as extra help as well as Jeb and he had everyone busy already. The schedule was full and he was conscious of trying to satisfy each and every customer. But information from the previous evening continued to swirl in his head.

Stace Grant was on his way into town. He'd had enough of Julie's griping for one day. Maybe he'd just stay away the entire day. That'd fix her alright. Always nagging him day after day. No man should have to put up with that, certainly not a fine upstanding guy like him.

Ever since that reporter lady had come to see him, he'd been uneasy, waking up in the middle of the night with that face before him. He thought there was something familiar about that girl, but he just couldn't wrap his mind around it. Well, she said she'd be back with more questions so maybe he'd be able to figure things out when she came back.

But she had brought back a whole lot of memories that Stace Grant would just as soon forget. Rarely did he think about the events of that night in 1942 anymore; but since the reporter's visit, he had been plagued by recurring nightmares.

Right now he was going to have a bit of breakfast and then maybe hang out at the garage awhile to see what was going on there.

Willow needed to talk to her mother about her discovery and wasn't sure just how that would go. Maybe tonight at the supper table would be a good time. Right now she needed to be on her way to take Grandpa Cain to his doctor's appointment then she was to have lunch with her mother on Eve's lunch break at work. And she had promised to bake a couple batches of brownies for the church ladies' bizarre coming up tomorrow. So it would be a full day for Willow. But it would probably end with Bobby coming over for a bit and that would be a reward at the end of a busy day. But presenting the evidence to her mother was first priority.

Someone had to have written that note if Chuck Evans hadn't.

As Stace entered the garage, Bobby's first thought was that he didn't have time today to shoot the breeze with Stace Grant. Most of the time when he dropped by he just wanted to talk a bit and brag on himself or complain about Julie or the heat or the cold or the city government or the federal government. Today was no exception but he mostly hovered around Jeb, perhaps sensing Bobby wanted to be left alone. Well, that would be okay with Bobby as long as Jeb kept working. Brian smiled at his big brother, being fully aware of how Bobby felt. It was mid-morning before Stace ambled over to where Bobby was working.

"Sure is a hot one taday, ain't it?" he tried to begin a conversation, perhaps sensing Bobby's unwillingness to carry on a conversation today.

"You remember that little reporter that was out to the house when you wuz there?" he continued.

Bobby grunted in response.

"You seen her around before?"

Bobby hesitated.

"Maybe."

"She sure looks familiar to me," Stace said pulling at his suspenders.

Bobby did not respond but kept working on the project at hand. So Stace turned his attention to other things around town. Ambling over to the bulletin board where people were free to post items of interest such as things for sale or rent or free kittens, he studied them carefully.

"Hey, Bobby, you got a pencil and paper?" he inquired, having evidently found something of interest.

"On the corner of my desk," Bobby replied, continuing to work on the car in front of him.

Stace stayed through the lunch hour and finally left about 1:30 apparently having satisfied his socialization for the day or perhaps had figured out that Julie may have cooled off and it was safe to return to the trailer.

Later that afternoon, as Bobby was giving the last cleanup of the day, he found the name and address on the scrap of paper

Stace had written on. It surely must not have been that important and Bobby dumped it in the wastebasket with the other trash for the day.

He was in a hurry to get over to Willow's house and needed to hit the shower first.

They sat across from each other at the table. Willow had gone ahead and prepared supper while she was working in the kitchen making brownies for the church bazaar. She finished putting the last bowl of food on the table while Eve changed clothes after work.

"Tired, Mom?" she asked.

Eve stretched and rubbed her forehead.

"Yeah, it's been a long day…and hot. Mr. Stevens did get a couple of fans for the office and that helps, but it's still hot. How was Grandpa's doctor's appointment?"

"Doctor said he was in pretty good shape. No changes in medication. Encouraged him to continue working outside. Said it was good for him, but to take it slower in the heat. And be sure to drink plenty of water."

Eve shook her head, indicating she understood.

"I appreciate you helping out with that."

"No problem, Mom."

They ate in silence for a while.

"Mom," Willow began, "could I see the poem Dad wrote to you one more time?"

Eve took time to take a drink of the ice water before she responded.

"I guess. It's in the wooden box you gave me for Christmas when you were a kid."

"Thanks."

Supper dishes were done, and Willow tried to suppress her overwhelming desire to run to the wooden box. After she thought a respectable amount of time had passed, she removed the poem; and taking the note once more from her purse, compared the two. Even the most inexperienced handwriting expert could see they were not written by the same person. But she thought maybe Tim O'Toole should take a look at it and perhaps there was someone down at the station who was an expert in the field.

She was right and all involved concurred that the handwriting was not the same. The suicide note indeed was not written by Chuck Evans. But who? Who would have written it and who would have done such a thing? And had an apparent suicide just become a murder?

Willow hurried to the garage. She needed to share the news with Bobby. He looked up from his paperwork while the impact wrench whined away in the work area.

"Hey, honey, what brings you down here?" he asked as he stood and gave her a good morning kiss.

"News," she beamed. "I've just come from the police station. Look."

And she removed the copies of the note and poem from her purse.

He studied them for a while.

"Whew," he breathed a low sound. "They sure aren't the same, are they?"

"Yes," she confirmed, "and Tim and the handwriting expert at the police station agree as well."

"What next?" he asked, turning towards her.

"Well, now we have to find out who wrote that note and right now my only lead is Stace Grant."

Bobby got a weird feeling in his stomach as things began to come together in his mind.

"Wait a minute," he became agitated.

He went to the bulletin board. No, there was nothing there, but still he wanted to look for something. Then he remembered. Stace Grant had copied something off the bulletin board…a name and address for something or other. But he had left it. Now, Bobby remembered seeing it and thinking it must not have been very important. But what had he done with it?"

"What's wrong with you?" Willow asked as she observed his restless behavior.

"Something clicked in my mind when you mentioned Stace Grant and then the writing. He was here yesterday and he wrote something down but he left it here. I remember seeing it, but what did I do with it?"

She helped him look.

Suddenly he remembered.

"The waste basket," he announced. "I think I threw it in the waste basket when I was cleaning up."

They both went to the barrel and found nothing. Bobby stood shaking his head in bewilderment. Rushing to his office, he grabbed the waste basket by his desk and shook its contents onto the floor. Finding the crumbled piece of paper he remembered, he handed it to Willow.

"Here it is. Does this match anything at all, Willow?"

It was their collective opinion that it did indeed. But, again, she needed more verification so she took the samples back to the police station. Yes, indeed, it was confirmed that the person who wrote the suicide note and the person who had written the address on the scrap of paper were one and the same.

"So whose handwriting was it?" Tim wanted to know.

Willow stuttered a bit.

"I have a hunch; but even though I think I know, I can't just accuse him, can I?"

"We need a confession."

"I need to think about this," was her final answer as she left the station.

Willow needed time to formulate a plan. One slip up at this stage could ruin everything.

She determined that she would wait until Stace Grant came into the garage again and then Bobby could call her and she in turn would call Tim O'Toole. Bobby was not at all at ease with her going out to the trailer or meeting him on her own. And Tim more or less agreed. Now, nothing to do but wait. Willow thought about what questions she might ask him to get the information they needed. Tim would have to stay in the background to prevent Stace from getting spooked. Everyone agreed he would feel most comfortable at the garage.

They waited. Day after day went by with no sign of Stace Grant. Then on a Tuesday in mid-July, Stace's old car pulled up in front of the garage. Bobby just happened to be at the door when he saw him and immediately went to his office to place the call to Willow. Taking a deep breath, he walked back into the work area.

"Mornin', Stace," he said, hoping his voice had not betrayed his nervousness.

"Hey."

"How's it goin'?"

"Like usual. You know how women are. Needed a break from her yappin'."

Here he took time to give out with a raucous laugh which spawned a fit of coughing.

"You okay?" Bobby asked out of concern.

"Chest," Stace said, grabbing at his chest. "It tightens up a bit now and then. Julie's cooking, I guess. She ain't much of a cook."

This was followed by another round of uncontrollable coughing.

Bobby watched Stace for the next few minutes, concluding Stace was continuing to have issues.

"Stace," he started, "you don't look so good. Are you sure you're alright? Here, come sit down."

"Can't breathe," Stace gasped for air.

Bobby flew into action, calling 911 with one hand while he loosened Stace's shirt from around his neck.

"Hang in there, buddy," he encouraged. "Help's on the way."

They arrived in minutes, but it seemed like an eternity.

Willow saw flashing lights up ahead as she rushed to the garage. They only increased the nervousness she felt. By the time she brought the car to a halt, ambulance personnel were hoisting Stace into the vehicle on a stretcher and Tim O'Toole was running from his car parked behind her. He outran her, reaching the ambulance just as they were closing the doors. Bobby stood nearby.

"What happened?" Willow asked, sensing Bobby's concern.

"I don't know," he answered. "He just came in and then he was holding his chest and then he said he couldn't breathe, so I called for help."

"Are you okay?" she said, touching his arm.

He rubbed one hand across the top of his head.

"Yeah, I guess so. I just hope he makes it."

The three of them arrived at the hospital in Tim's cruiser only minutes behind the ambulance. Pushing their way past hospital staff, Tim flashed his badge and asked a few questions. Returning to Willow and Bobby, he shared the bit of news: Stace Grant was unresponsive.

They waited. A policeman, who had obviously been sent to get her, escorted Julie Grant into the waiting room. Willow stood and introduced herself simply as Willow and told her how sorry she was and that she was just on her way to conduct an interview with Stace when the horrible tragedy had taken place. Her sympathy was genuine and genuinely accepted. Julie thanked her and acknowledged Bobby standing there.

They sat in silence and waited. People in white coats and nurses in white dresses, caps, shoes and hose glided through the halls in silence, carrying out their duties with efficiency. People whispered in low tones and somewhere a baby was crying. Bobby held Willow's hand to keep her from shaking; and besides, holding her hand quieted his own nerves as well. Tim paced the floor and frequently stopped someone in the hallway to ask if there was any news.

Finally, a dark haired man in a white coat approached and Julie Grant stood.

"Mrs. Grant?" the doctor addressed her.

Julie put her handkerchief to her face, bracing herself for the news.

"He's stable now," the doctor said. "It was a close call and he needs to just be quiet and rest. You can go in to see him, but just for a few minutes; and please, do not say anything that would upset him. The next twenty four to forty eight hours are critical."

With those words, he touched her gently on the shoulder and turned to engage in the next emergency.

Julie followed the nurse towards the darkened room and the three sat looking at each other.

"It doesn't look like there's any more to be done here tonight," Tim said. "If he pulls through, then we can talk to him."

Chapter Fourteen

August loomed ahead. The summer was passing by too quickly and Willow felt she was at a standstill in her quest for the truth about her father's death. And now Stace Grant was confined to a hospital bed and she hadn't been able to get to him to ask him all the questions that still were unanswered. Then there was the matter of returning to school in about three weeks.

But it had been a good summer all in all. Her issues with Scott had been resolved, she'd been able to spend time with her mother and family and then there was Bobby. Who would have believed this summer would have ended up with her falling in love? And she most certainly was in love.

When she thought of that, a tingling sensation rushed throughout her body. Recalling his eyes that day in the restaurant, feeling the firmness of his shoulders when they had danced together, his strength when they swam at the lake, the compassion he exhibited in helping Clem...all were engraved in her memory. Yes, there was no doubt in her mind that Willow Evans was in love with Bobby Carson. The revelation caused her do a dance twirl around her mother's kitchen.

The celebration of love was interrupted by the sound of the phone ringing.

"Hello."

"Willow, come quick."

"Alice, is that you?"

It was. Alice was in trouble with her pregnancy and Willow was out the door in seconds, exceeding the speed limit to get to her. After putting the little ones in the care of a neighbor, she loaded Alice into the car and headed for the hospital.

Didn't it seem as if she was just here at this place with the Stace Grant crises? She prayed that Alice and the baby would be okay and was relieved when the doctor's report was favorable. Alice would be fine and from all indications, the baby appeared to be unharmed. However, Alice would be in the hospital a few days for observation and rest. And didn't Willow know the nurses would have their hands full.

Willow smoothed back the hair of her best friend as she lay still against the white sheets. Alice opened her eyes.

"I'm glad you're here," she murmured. "Thanks, Willow...for getting me here...for being my best friend."

Tears came to her eyes and Willow squeezed her hand.

"You're going to be fine," Willow encouraged. "The doctor says you just need a bit of rest."

"Better call Frank," Alice whispered. "Try not to alarm him."

Yeah, right. There was no doubt in Willow's mind what Frank's reaction would be with the news that his wife and unborn child were in the hospital.

"And tell him I need something chocolate!" she called as Willow was walking out the door.

"I'm going to run up to the hospital and visit a bit with Alice," Willow told Bobby.

"If you don't mind, I'll go with you," he said. "I need to check in on Stace to see if there's been any change."

So it was that Willow and Bobby entered the hospital. With a bouquet of flowers in her hand, Willow braced herself for the unexpected, but Alice was sitting up in bed and looking a whole lot better than she had a couple days earlier. After seeing that Alice was doing alright and leaving the two girls to chat, Bobby excused himself to go down the hallway to another wing of the hospital to locate Room 312...Stace Grant's room. But he wasn't the only visitor this evening. Tim O'Toole was making a hospital call as well.

The nurse on duty told them Stace Grant had been drifting back and forth between periods of ranting alternating with periods of lucidity; and with that, she left them alone in the room with the patient.

The nurse was correct. Sometimes Stace lay very still and quiet and sometimes he became agitated and was very vocal although usually unintelligible. Tim moved to one side of the bed and Bobby stood on the opposite side, both straining their ears to pick up any bits of information Stace might utter. They had been there for maybe fifteen minutes or more when Willow found her way down the hallway to Room 312. The room was dark except for the light above Stace's bed. It was evening and the nurse had pulled the drapes over the window so light in the room was subdued at best. But it was sufficient to cast enough shadow over Willow's face…enough to cloud Stace's vision. Willow quietly approached the foot of the bed, just ready to inquire if there was any change. She stopped abruptly when Stace chose that particular moment to sit straight up and open his eyes. At first it was as if he didn't focus on anything and then he seemed to concentrate wholly on the figure standing straight ahead of him.

"It's you! I knew you'd come sooner or later," he called out in a clear voice, staring with wild eyes.

Willow's first inclination was to panic and run back into the hallway.

Both men looked helplessly at Willow. Tim made signs for her to engage in conversation. A quick look at Bobby encouraged her with a nod.

"I…I'm here," she said, her voice quivering.

"I knew you'd come back, come back to haunt me!"

Willow grasped for ideas.

"Why would you think that?"

" 'Cause of what I done," Stace was becoming emotional.

"What did you do, Stace?"

He was visibly shaken and restless, pulling at the bed sheets.

"I didn't mean it, Chuck. Honest I didn't."

Realizing that her remarkable resemblance to her father combined with the dim lighting and the circumstances had triggered his memory, Willow proceeded with more confidence.

"What is it you did, buddy?"

Somehow she thought familiarity was the best way to go.

"That night. That night of the accident. I'm sorry. I'm so sorry!"

He began to sob.

Willow pressed forward.

"What happened that night?"

"No, no! I can't go there. It's too painful."

"It's okay. A strong man like you can do it. I know you can do it."

Stace shook his head, but never once took his eyes off the figure at the foot of his bed.

She had to ask the question.

"Did you kill me, Stace?"

"Oh, no," he whined, "I couldn't do that. It was the note."

"What about the note?"

"It was me. I wrote it!"

Tim motioned for Willow to keep pressing him.

"But, why, Stace? Why would *you* write a suicide note?"

"I could have been a war hero. I could have made Eve a good husband. But she wanted you and I just wanted to get even."

He continued to be emotional, tears streaming down his face now.

Willow grabbed the end of the bed with both hands to keep her knees from buckling from underneath her. Her voice now was quivering and weak. For one brief moment she remembered the doctor's words about not upsetting him, yet she needed to hear all of the story.

"How did it happen, Stace? It's okay. Now you can finally tell the whole truth."

Stace's face contorted and his voice was low and controlled.

"I left right after you did and followed you that night and caught up with you just in time to see the car go over the edge. I hurried down the hill but you wuz already dead. I knew that right away when I got there. And then I got this idea. So I just grabbed a paper and wrote the note. I thought it wouldn't make any difference 'cause you wuz already dead."

He was agonizing now, still totally oblivious to the other two men in the room.

"I'm sorry. I knew it was wrong. I don't know why I did it. I'm so sorry."

He was sobbing now and his breaths were coming in gasps.

Compassion overcame Willow as tears trickled down her own cheeks.

"It's okay, Stace. You did the right thing in telling me. You did the right thing," she added softly.

It was as if her words finally had rid Stace of the burden he had carried for so long. He collapsed on the pillow and appeared to be finally in a restful sleep.

Bobby rushed to Willow's side quickly enough to hold Willow's collapsing body in his arms.

Tim O'Toole was running on adrenalin.

"That's it! That's all we needed to hear. Good job, Willow," he commended. "That will do. And I know just the right person to contact at the newspaper."

With that, Tim was out the door.

Willow and Bobby walked slowly down the hallway, both too overwhelmed by the events of the evening to find words.

They were all assembled in Eve Evans' home…Eve, Willow, Aunt Flo and Uncle Gage, Uncle Zach and Sally and Grandpa Cain. Willow related the entire story and there were various reactions. Eve cried. Uncle Zach thought Stace Grant should be put in jail forever. Grandpa Cain just wanted to share the news with Grandma Cain.

Willow patted his shoulder.

"I'd like to think she already knows," she said softly.

After everyone was gone and just Eve and Willow remained sitting in the living room, Willow spoke softly to her mother.

"You know what I need to do," she said.

"I know. They should know."

Willow needed to share the news with two other people.

Again, Willow was once again sitting in her car across from the small blue house with the white shutters just like she had earlier in the summer when she observed Charles Evans getting his morning newspaper from the mailbox. She hoped she would have the opportunity to share her news with them. How could she ever hope to replace the hurt that had festered for all this time? Understanding this visit could very well end up in rejection, she knew it was something she had to do. Somehow it would be worth the risk. Reaching for the door handle, she grabbed the newspaper which had been published with the story clarifying the details of the accident and left her car and walked across the street, up the walk and rang the doorbell. It was an agonizing few seconds before the door opened and a small woman with a friendly face peered at her through a pair of eye glasses.

"Yes?"

"Nancy Evans?"

"Yes."

"I'm Willow and I need to talk to you."

Nancy Evans drew in a hurried breath and glanced around over her shoulder as she stepped back away from the door so Willow could step inside.

"Come in."

"I have news," Willow said as she closed the door behind her.

She saw the distress in Nancy Evans' face.

"No, no," she attempted to explain. "I think you'll find it good news."

"Who is it, Nancy?"

The tall, good-looking gentleman Willow had seen earlier in the summer entered the room. He stopped short and a mixture of pain and anger came across his face. The shock of brown curls, those eyes. Charles Evans did not need ask who their guest was.

Nancy turned towards her husband.

"This is Willow, Charles. She says she has news."

"I don't want to hear any news."

And Charles Evans turned to leave.

"Sit down, won't you?" Nancy said as she gestured towards a chair, sending a look of concern after her husband.

Willow sat down cautiously, took a deep breath and began her story, starting with her early curiosity about her father's death. Nancy Evans situated herself in a chair across the room and Charles Evans stood in the doorway to the living room, not willing to be a part of the conversation, but just curious enough to be comfortably detached from it. As the story unfolded, he moved closer and eventually sat on the sofa near Willow's chair. At the end of the saga and the presentation of the newspaper, tears had replaced the denial on Charles Evans' face. When Willow looked into his eyes, she saw the same thing she saw when she looked at herself in a mirror.

Well, she had come to say what she had to say. The rest would be up to Charles and Nancy Evans. So she stood to leave. Nancy was the first to respond. Gathering Willow in her arms, she held her tightly.

"I'm so glad you came, my dear," she whispered. "It's been a lonely life since the accident."

Willow attempted to respond when she felt a pair of strong arms encircling them both. A lifetime of sadness was being washed away. As she walked across the street and started her car, Willow knew that it would take some time, but she would indeed have another set of grandparents in her life and the healing process had already begun. She turned to smile and wave at the figures standing in the doorway to the little blue house with the white shutters. What a difference a few minutes can make in the course of one's life.

Eve stood before the mirror in her bathroom. Willow was off to Graceville to tell Chuck's parents that his death was indeed not a suicide, but an accident. Stace Grant had taken advantage of the situation by writing the note in an attempt at revenge for Eve's rejection of him and his rejection at the chance to serve in the army. For a moment she thought she could picture Chuck's reflection in the mirror beside her.

"Oh, Chuck," she murmured out loud, "you'd be so proud of our little girl. She has cleared your name after all this time. She is truly amazing…our little girl."

He was standing at the bathroom sink, face lathered and razor in hand. Eve approached behind him. She did so enjoy watching him shave.

"She's amazing, you know," Eve said as she put her arms around him.

He made a stroke of the razor up the side of his neck and then swished it in the basin of water.

"Just like her mother," he admired.

"And her father," she reminded him.

"What kind of person do you think she'll grow up to be?"

He took time to finish shaving the rest of his neck before he spoke.

"Someone great, I imagine. I don't know if she'll be a teacher or a lawyer or president of the United States, but I just want her to be a good person…kind, compassionate, respected by others. That's what I want for our little girl."

"And what of her little brother?" Eve teased.

Chuck stopped the shaving and looked at his wife's mirror reflection in surprise.

"Are you trying to tell me something?"

"I don't know for sure. But I think so."

He felt her arms around him, caressing his chest. He whirled around and grabbed her, kissing her, smearing shaving cream all over her face. But she didn't mind at all. She relished his love.

Afterwards she pulled the sheets around her as she lay there while he shaved and whistled in the bathroom.

"I love you, Chuck Evans," she said aloud.

"I heard that," he called from the bathroom. "And I love you, Evie Joanne."

The timing for the pregnancy had been bad. News of Chuck's death was so traumatic to her body, that she miscarried and lost the baby. She had dealt with double loss then, but it resurfaced now and Eve Evans gave way to the sorrow she carried. Tears fell freely as she sobbed until she felt drained of emotion. Willow should be back soon and she needed to be presentable. After all, no one had ever known about the baby…not her mother or sister Flo. No one except her family doctor.

Willow called Bobby just as soon as she returned to tell him of her visit with Grandfather and Grandmother Evans. He listened without interrupting her, realizing she needed to get the entire story out.

"So Mom and I are taking a couple of days and are going out of town," she told him.

"I'll miss you, but I understand."

"I'll miss you, too. We have a lot to talk about. I'll call you when I get back."

He thought about her words while she was gone the two days. Was he reading something into them that wasn't there? He was totally aware that the summer was coming to a close and knew what that could mean. Willow would soon be going back to college. But what did that mean for them? To all they'd experienced and felt through the summer? Well, he would just have to wait to see what she had in mind.

Two days seemed like an eternity. But Bobby was busy. He had some shopping to do and some plans to make. He wanted to be ready when Willow returned and called him.

It was a good couple of days for mother and daughter. They relaxed and walked and talked and ate at a nice restaurant. Eve viewed her daughter with pride and Willow shared all the events of the summer and her feelings for Bobby. And was Eve surprised? Not at all. In some small way, she saw their relationship similar to that of Chuck and herself. Could she want any more for her daughter?

It had been a wonderful summer, putting to rest many issues.

It was Saturday and Bobby closed the garage at noon. Jeb didn't think he'd ever remembered Bobby closing that early. But Bobby had things to do. Everything had to be just perfect. He gathered, he shopped, he prepared, all the while visions of Willow dancing through his head. Memories of the summer flooded his mind…talking with her at the funeral home when they hadn't seen each other for three years or so, sitting in the stands at his baseball games in those white shorts, laughing with him, talking to him, inspiring him.

He had told her to be there at 7:30 and he could hardly wait. The anticipation was overwhelming. Once everything was in place, he showered and spent extra time picking out his clothes. What on earth had come over him? Since when had these things become so important to him? But this evening had to be perfect. It just *had* to be.

He told her 7:30. So why was she still trying to decide what to wear at 7:15? If she didn't snap into high gear, she most certainly would be late. And she didn't want to be late. He had made it sound like such a special evening. And she wanted it to be special. With the mystery surrounding her father's death put to rest and her relationship with Scott resolved, and the summer pretty much behind her now, it was time to rest and enjoy herself. Thoughts of the summer activities being almost over caused her to feel apprehension. At one time, graduation from college had just been something out there in the future. Now it was looming before her and decisions would have to be made.

She finally chose the sundress she and Aunt Flo had picked up on sale earlier in the summer. It had a solid pale blue top which gave way to a blue and white checked skirt. It was decorated with white buttons and a bow in the back. Willow admired her tan. She really had gotten some sun this summer. Debating between white heels or flats, the white flats won the debate since she was unsure of the evening's activities. Tiny white earrings were a good choice as well as a matching beaded bracelet. Should she have worn shorts? It was a last minute thought. Bobby said to meet him down by the creek. Maybe shorts would have been a better choice. But he also said something else that made her think she should maybe dress up a bit. Too late to change now, she thought. She needed to be out the door.

He had been there for an hour, fussing over everything he had planned. He checked his watch frequently and wondered if his light blue shirt and navy slacks were appropriate. He breathed easier when he heard her car up on the road. Time to do the last minute preparations.

Music coming through the night air was the first thing she heard. Strains of Elvis' *Love Me Tender* floated through the August evening. As she walked towards the creek, she saw the table, complete with white table cloth, fresh flowers and blue candles showing up against the darkening skies. It took her breath away. Upon closer inspection, she noticed the table was set for two. A small gift was wrapped in silver paper with a blue bow and there was a note on one of the plates. Written in bold lettering was the word *Willow.* She picked it up and opened it.

To the girl who has made this the most wonderful summer of my life,
Thank you for being so special and caring.
Welcome to a world of love.
If you don't share those feelings, walk away now.
If you do share those feelings, give me a sign.

She folded the note and placed it back on the table. At first he thought perhaps she was going to refuse the invitation; but instead, she whirled around and yelled.

"I *do* share those feelings! I *do*!"

It was then he came out from his hiding place among the trees. They met each other half way and he grabbed her and held her close, then kissed her and she responded. They stood there lost in the magic of their love.

"How about some dinner, princess?" he murmured.

"Dinner, too?" she smiled.

"You ain't seen nothing' yet," he called over his shoulder as he fumbled in boxes and coolers and placed his culinary achievements before her. They talked and teased and laughed until the last piece of dessert was consumed and darkness was settling in for the night.

"You said we needed to talk."

"Yes, I guess I did say that."

She was quiet and he felt an uncomfortableness come over him.

"School," she said.

"What about it?" he asked.

"Less than two weeks away."

She sounded sad.

"What do you think we should do about that?"

"I don't know," she walked away from him a bit.

She continued.

"I'm confused," she tried to explain. "I want to be a teacher. I've always wanted to be a teacher, but this summer has shown me that I want some other things in life as well."

She was conscious that he was moving back to the table. He returned to her side with the small box.

"Perhaps this will help you make up your mind," he said softly.

She looked at him with questions in her eyes and then pulled at the blue bow, slowly releasing the silver wrapping. Opening the box with great care, she gasped at its contents. A ring. A sparkling diamond set in silver.

"Oh, Bobby!" she gasped.

"Willow Evans," he said softly as he took her hand in his, "I have loved you for so long. Will you put me out of my misery and marry me?"

"Oh, yes, yes, yes!" she screamed as she threw her arms around his neck.

He was kissing her; she responded to him. More happiness than either of them had ever known flooded their bodies. They stood gazing into each other's eyes.

"I guess we do have a lot to talk about," he began. "First of all, I want you to finish your education. We will work something out, some way to see each other. I can come up some weekends, if that's okay with you."

"And I can come home some weekends," she added. "Plus I will start looking for openings in this area for teaching positions."

"Are you sure?" he asked. "I want you to be satisfied with your choices. I can always start a garage somewhere else."

"No, I'll find a job somewhere close by. You already have your business established. Besides, with Mom and Grandpa and the rest of the family here, a job close by would be perfect."

"It will be good for you to be close to your mother while you plan the wedding," he murmured.

"A wedding."

She was thrilled. A wedding.

"How about just as soon as you graduate from college in the spring?" he suggested.

"Can we wait that long?" she smiled.

"With you at the end of the rainbow…well, it will be hard…but we can do it."

"What a wonderful future…together."

"And we can start looking for houses," he planned. "Ever since you bought that welcome sign at the Fourth of July celebration, I've pictured us together in our own home."

She hugged him tight.

"Make it big enough for a big family," she whispered.

He kissed her.

"Just what I was thinkin'."

They gathered up the dinner things as they continued to plan. The moon climbed up the eastern sky and began to drift above them.

"It's perfect," she said, looking up.

"You're perfect, Willow," he whispered. "Just like that Willow tree…bending but never breaking. Always graceful, always strong."

There was one last place Willow needed to visit before she put things to rest. Driving slowly through the gravel paths, she wound her way past granite stones. Pausing near Grandma Cain's resting place, she felt peace there, taking time to note the Mason jar filled with fresh flowers. Obviously Grandpa Cain had been up early that morning. A smile passed across her face at Grandpa's continued thoughtfulness. The car moved slowly, inching its way around the curves perhaps out of respect for the deceased until Willow saw the stone she searched for. Stopping the car, she opened the door; and taking the spray of flowers from the seat next to her, she walked across the drying grass towards the marble stone. It was a calm August day. Not a single breeze played in the tops of the trees. All was quiet except for the dull buzz of katydids predicting the coming of autumn.

She placed the flowers at the base of the stone next to his name and sat cross legged in front of it. Reaching over, she gently brushed away the dried grass clippings from the last mowing. Seemingly satisfied with that, she sat quietly for the longest time.

"I did it, Dad," she whispered. "I finally found out the truth. And now I know that you never intended to leave us, you never wanted to leave us and that you loved us very much. That's important to me."

She sat back and gave an audible sigh before she continued.

"I hope you approve and I think you do. I felt you whisper my name at the crash site. It sure has made me feel a lot better to know the truth."

Another pause.

"And I hope you didn't suffer much in the crash."

She choked with emotion.

"Mom has suffered a lot since then, but I think you already know that."

She dug in her pocket for a handkerchief and wiped her eyes and blew her nose.

"I visited Grandpa and Grandma Evans and I think they will be coming around now, so you quite possibly might expect to see them coming by here for a visit."

After spending more quiet time reflecting on the few memories she still had of him, she stood to leave.

"Oh, yeah, this summer I think I've found the perfect man for my life. I *know* I have. I think Mom approves 'cause she sees some of the happiness in me that she had with you."

Again, she stood quietly for some time.

"I love you, Daddy."

She gently touched his tombstone in a gesture of goodbye.

And then, just as she had experienced at the site of the crash, she heard a small whisper as if someone was calling her name and felt a slight movement on her cheek. Looking skyward proved to her there wasn't a breeze anywhere around, nothing stirring. She touched her face and felt the spot. Turning back towards the grave, she smiled.

"Thank you, Daddy."

- The End -

Books by G.L. Gracie

Amelia

The Rose Trilogy:

Ivy and Wild Roses

Sweet Primrose

The White Rose

Willow

Refuge From the Storm

Coming in 2015

When Magnolias Bloom

Made in the USA
Charleston, SC
16 September 2015